BETTER THAN THE CAVALRY

Fargo fired the Colt from where he leaned against the Ovaro, saw the man's bald head erupt in a shower of scarlet as he turned into a grotesque, bulbous figure with something that resembled a giant beet atop it. Fighting off another wave of dizziness, Fargo pulled himself onto the horse, heard his groan of pain, and felt Mei Ling's hands helping him. She climbed onto the horse behind him as he swept Baldy's men with the Colt. They didn't move, their eyes fixed on the grotesque, lifeless figure. Fargo sent the Ovaro into a trot, rode through the onlookers that parted for him, fought away more waves of pain-filled dizziness, and rode from the town in the last light of the day.

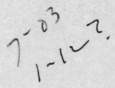

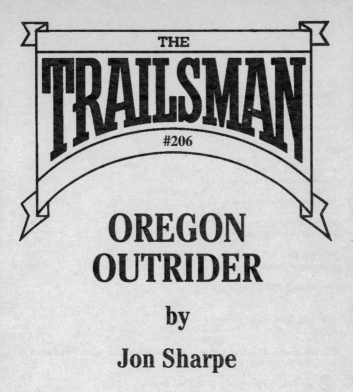

THE
TRAILSMAN

#206

OREGON
OUTRIDER

by

Jon Sharpe

A SIGNET BOOK

SIGNET
Published by the Penguin Group
Penguin Putnam Inc., 375 Hudson Street,
New York, New York 10014, U.S.A.
Penguin Books Ltd, 27 Wrights Lane,
London W8 5TZ, England
Penguin Books Australia Ltd,
Ringwood, Victoria, Australia
Penguin Books Canada Ltd, 10 Alcorn Avenue,
Toronto, Ontario, Canada M4V 3B2
Penguin Books (N.Z.) Ltd, 182–190 Wairau Road,
Auckland 10, New Zealand

Penguin Books Ltd, Registered Offices:
Harmondsworth, Middlesex, England

First published by Signet, an imprint of Dutton NAL,
a member of Penguin Putnam Inc.

First Printing, January, 1999
10 9 8 7 6 5 4 3 2 1

The first chapter of this book originally appeared in *Mountain Mankillers*, the two
hundred-fifth volume of this series.

   REGISTERED TRADEMARK—MARCA REGISTRADA

Printed in the United States of America

The Trailsman

Beginnings . . . they bend the tree and they mark the man. Skye Fargo was born when he was eighteen. Terror was his midwife, vengeance his first cry. Killing spawned Skye Fargo, ruthless, cold-blooded murder. Out of the acrid smoke of gunpowder still hanging in the air, he rose, cried out a promise never forgotten.

The Trailsman they began to call him all across the West: searcher, scout, hunter, the man who could see where others only looked, his skills for hire but not his soul, the man who lived each day to the fullest, yet trailed each tomorrow. Skye Fargo, the Trailsman, and the seeker who could take the wildness of a land and the wanting of a woman and make them his own.

1860, the far land of Oregon beckoned like a rainbow at the end of the long trail of suffering and hardship. But to many, the rainbow was an illusion, their only reward deceit, deception, new suffering, and living death. . . .

1

The three-masted barkentine had already become a two-masted vessel with the first strike of the screaming wind, but it was the towering mountain of seawater that snapped the mainmast as if it were a matchstick. Ten of the crew were swept overboard as they were whipped by torn halyards, clew lines, braces, and rigging ropes that curled around each man with a deadly embrace. Left only with a foremast, the ship rolled helplessly in the raging sea. The rock-strewn shore of the Oregon coastline was lighted by the flashes of lightning that tore the black night sky open.

The towering rocks seemed to rise up with a deadly promise as they waited with malevolent patience for their victims. The ship heeled far to the port side as another massive wave struck her and, when she slowly righted, the captain regained his feet on the stern deck. "The goddamn upper topsail," he screamed to the struggling figures below. "Secure the topgallant, too." Captain Juan Consalve cursed again as his battered ship shuddered under the impact of another tremendous wave. A short man with a pushed-in face, wrapped in his oilskins, he looked more like a toad than a person. His first mate, a lean, gangly figured man, pulled himself closer along the rail and the captain pointed to a crewman huddled against the rail. The sailor knelt on both knees, his head bowed, his hands held out together in prayer. "What the hell is he doing?" Captain Consalve screamed.

"He's praying. He won't move," the mate shouted back.

"Kick his ass," Juan Consalve roared back. "Get him to the foremast."

"He won't go. He's asking forgiveness. He says the storm is punishment for what we are doing," the mate said. The captain saw two crewmen halt and stare at the kneeling figure. Pulling a heavy Bentley percussion five-shot pistol from under his oilskins, he steadied himself against the pitch of the ship and fired off two shots. The praying crewman fell over dead and was immediately swept along the deck by a breaking wave. The other two crewmen tore their eyes away from the sight and ran to the foremast. Juan Consalve pocketed the pistol in satisfaction. He couldn't have the crew getting ideas about praying for salvation. He wanted only their muscles and bodies working to keep the ship afloat. They'd have time for praying if they were swept overboard.

The thought had just left the captain's mind when another terrible gust of wind sent his vessel heeling to port again. As he clung to the stern rail he saw a mountain of seawater join the wind to tear away all the sails on the foremast except the upper and lower topgallants. Trailing broken yardarms, shredded canvas, ropes, blocks, and assorted shrouds, the sails washed out into the churning sea. With only two sails left on the remaining mast, the ship was propelled helplessly by the raging wind. "Lower the boats," Juan Consalve shouted to his first mate.

"In these seas?" the mate questioned.

The captain pointed to the rocks. "You want to stay with the ship?" he asked. "It's hitting the rocks for sure. We've a chance with the boats." The mate nodded and started to hurry away. "Wait," the captain called. "Go down to the hold. Bring up the girl . . . the Peking merchant's daughter. She'll bring enough to buy us a new ship."

"What about the others?"

"Leave them."

"Tied up?"

"You want them fighting us for the boats?" Consalve said. The mate nodded and fought his way along the rolling deck, well aware the vessel carried only two lifeboats. The captain grimaced as he saw the spray-drenched rocks just ahead of the vessel. They'd do better riding the surface of the churning sea in the two lifeboats, he knew. Unlike the ship, the lifeboats had a chance to skirt their way between the rocks. But he was sweating inside his oilskins, fear gripping his short, squat form, his lips drawn back as he saw the ship being hurled directly at a huge rock. The mate reappeared, dragging a slender figure in a gray, one-piece dress. "Lower the boats," the captain shouted as he swung down to the main deck and felt the ship gather speed atop a towering wave.

The young woman pushed jet black wet hair from her face. "There are two hundred people tied belowdecks. They'll drown when we hit the rocks," she said.

"Most of them. Some might make it. We'll get any who do," Juan Consalve said.

The young woman struck out and tried to rake her nails across his pushed-in face. "Monster," she screamed. But he caught her arm and flung her to the deck.

The mate picked her up and pulled her to where the two lifeboats were being lowered, throwing her into the first one as if she were a sack of potatoes. Captain Juan Consalve fought through a drenching blast of seawater to reach the lifeboat, which was already filled with crew members. The black-haired young woman lay on the floor of the lifeboat as he knelt beside her and barked orders at the six crewmen manning the oars. The boat was lowered and immediately swept up atop a churning wave. "Row for the rocks," the captain shouted. "I'll tell you when to turn." Clutching the gunwale of the lifeboat with both hands, the captain peered through the wind and water, letting a lightning flash show him the two rocks dead ahead. He waited, lips drawn back, as the sea swept the boat in a sudden rush toward the rocks. "Now, now. Turn, goddamn it, turn," he shouted. The crewmen pulled hard on the oars, dug paddles into the top of churning waves, but with excruciating slowness, the boat began to turn.

There was a space behind the first towering rock, the captain had already seen, and now the lifeboat came abreast of it. With a little luck, they could slip through, he saw, grabbing the oar of the nearest crewman and pulling along with him. The sea cooperated, lifting the boat and sending it swirling through the space between the rocks, sending it racing toward a smaller, lower line of rocks. They'd hit and be tossed into the swirling sea, but not with the force that they'd avoided. Juan Consalve firmly believed in the triumph of evil over good. He had spent a lifetime working to prove that.

The big man with the lake blue eyes sat quietly inside the cave, warm and dry. He had seen the storm coming a little before dusk and sent his Ovaro into a fast trot as he rode a few thousand yards behind the Oregon coastline. He had seen these fierce storms sweep the coast, knew the total fury of their terrible power and he sent the horse into a canter as he searched for a place of safety. Only an hour before the storm struck, he found the cave. It was well within sight of the coast, and tall enough to accommodate the pinto. He rode in, unsaddled the horse, and stood at the mouth of the cave to see the sea already pounding the rocks of the shore. The wind and the rain quickly followed, and became a howling chorus as night fell. He turned back and found enough pieces of dry wood to make a small fire as the wind and the rain grew louder.

He was grateful he had found the cave, which was part of the area called the Devil's Elbow, a rugged, thickly forested part of the Oregon coast he had only ridden once before. He munched on a strip of cold beef jerky and listened to the howl of the storm grow louder. Rising, he stood at the mouth of the cave and peered out into the night. A tremendous flash of lightning turned night into day for a second, long enough to let him see what was left of a ship heading for the rocks. Another lightning flash showed the vessel had but one mast left.

The wind and driving seas were hurling it straight at the rocks.

Skye Fargo's lips drew back in a grimace. Those still aboard the ship had little chance for survival. They'd pay the price for hugging the Oregon coastline to save a few precious weeks. They all tried that, now. But it wasn't always so, he remembered, before gold was discovered in California in forty-nine. From there, gold fever quickly spread into Oregon. Not many ships sailed the Oregon coastline before that event, a few American hide droghers, wood vessels from Australia, frozen meat ships from New Zealand, and some small South American traders. But after the discovery of gold, a stream of British merchantmen, French barkentines, Portuguese schooners, and American clippers sailed the Oregon coast. The wreck in the darkness in front of him was just the latest of many and as he watched, another flash of lightning let him see the vessel smash into the rocks. It shuddered, then came apart in all directions.

The dark flooded back again and the wind screamed but he could hear the shattering of wood. Then, through the howl of the wind, he heard another sound, the scream of human voices somehow rising above the din of the storm. He squinted through the blackness. He could still hear the cries. Waiting, he peered hard, straining his eyes, but the lightning flashes grew less frequent. He could catch the sounds but he couldn't see the bodies tossed into the air by the tremendous waves. He could not see how, tied together, they were sent whirling through the air as if part of some grotesque daisy chain. Finally, the sounds faded and he retreated into the cave, where he lay down and catnapped till the silence woke him.

The storm had ended and Fargo rose to his feet. Stepping to the entrance of the cave, he peered out toward the shore where the moon had come out to linger at the edge of the horizon. The night neared an end, the moonlight a pale glow on the rocks and the broken remains of the ship. The first tint of dawn touched the distant sky soon afterward and he waited, watching until the new day began to spread itself across the scene. The seas still raged but the rest of the scene held an eerie peacefulness under the new sun, only the turbulent seas and the shattered ship's hulk any evidence that the storm had struck. Suddenly Fargo found himself leaning forward as he caught a glimpse of movement along the shoreline. He picked out figures along the sand and the rocks. They moved back and forth, plainly searching. Survivors searching for their comrades, a scene made of hope and drawn in poignancy.

Turning, Fargo went into the cave, saddled the Ovaro, and slowly rode into the open. He'd help them search. It was the least he could do. He let the pinto pick its way along the still slippery terrain toward the shore, the horse stepping carefully among the rocks, tough shore brush, wide patches of yellow-orange agoseris, reminiscent of dandelion but much hardier, and growths of thick-leafed, fernlike plants. Beyond lay the wet, hard-packed sand of the beach and beyond that, the rocks where the ship had been impaled. Fargo's eyes went to figures combing the rocks this side of the beach and he counted at least seven figures searching, then spied another group of five tied together with a length of rope. Two more figures stood with them.

The pinto skirted a flat rock when the horse halted and then reared back. "Easy," Fargo murmured, his eyes going to the patch of wide-leafed shore growth that lay still flattened by the force of the rain that had deluged them. He urged the pinto forward but once again the horse refused and backed away. Long ago, Fargo had learned to trust that instinctive wisdom, the special sixth sense animals possessed beyond anything humans could muster. Drawing the Colt at his hip, he dismounted and pushed the thick-leafed brush back with his foot. His eyes widened as he looked down at the slender figure that lay beneath the brush. Jet black hair, cut short, finely formed features, and eyes black and almond-shaped, she stared up at him from a face of delicate Oriental beauty. Chinese, he guessed, from the fine formation of her high cheekbones. But it was the expression in her jet eyes that held him, a terrible pleading made of fear, desperation, and a fierce anger that glittered through everything else. He frowned at her wet form, her body curled up into a fetal position. She made no sound but her eyes pleaded for help, crying out for him not to reveal she was there.

Fargo let the thick fronds fall back into place and the slender figure disappeared from sight under them. The frown dug hard into his brow as he led the pinto forward and skirted the spot as questions whirled through his mind. Had the girl been aboard the ship? If so, why was she hiding? Survivors didn't hide. Or was she something other than a survivor? Was she on her own, no part of the wrecked ship? The question asked itself again. Why was she hiding, so clearly fearful of being discovered? The frown was still digging into his brow as he reached the first line of rocks before the wide beach. A short, squat but powerfully built figure wearing a captain's cap and uniform, barked orders to the seven men combing the rocks. Fargo's eyes went to the five figures that were tied together and saw each wore wrist irons. The two men with them carried rifles, he noted. And he noted something else. The five shackled figures were all Chinese.

A strange uneasiness began to creep through him as he moved closer and the man in the captain's uniform turned and came toward him. Fargo took in a pushed-in face, small eyes, and thick lips. "You from the ship?" Fargo asked.

"*Sim.* Captain Juan Consalve," the man said, his accent very Portuguese.

"Portuguese trader?" Fargo questioned.

"*Sim.*" The man nodded.

"Came down to see if I could help. Didn't think there'd be anyone left alive," Fargo said.

"A few of us survived," the captain said.

Fargo's eyes went to the five shackled figures. "Why the wrist irons?" he queried.

"Prisoners, from your jails. We were taking them back when the storm hit," Consalve said. Fargo's glance stayed on the five men. All were plainly Chinese and none wore prison uniforms, though that didn't mean a lot in and of itself. Yet the fact clung inside him.

"All prisoners and all Chinese," Fargo remarked casually. "Kind of strange." His casual tone belied the sharpness in his lake blue eyes. The captain paused, plainly searching for an answer.

"They were all part of a gang," he said, finally.

Fargo nodded, smiling inwardly. The captain had the smarts to think quickly, his answer both plausible and reasonable, yet stretching probability. Fargo couldn't dismiss it but a warning pushed at him and the image of a fearful young Chinese girl hiding under the wet fronds flashed through his mind. Something was not quite in order in this scene of shattered ship and drowned passengers. Did the terrible storm hide evil inside tragedy? The thought lay in his mind as he moved the pinto a step backward. "I'll search some on my own. Might just find some more survivors," Fargo said.

"Whatever help you can give us," the captain said. "Call us if you find anyone."

"Sure thing," Fargo agreed and sent the Ovaro at a slow walk along the wet rocks, his eyes sweeping the terrain, the barnacle-covered rocks, the flat sand, and the creviced coastal ridges. The sun warmed the earth, bringing out the brilliant beauty in pods of starfish as it glinted on barely submerged beds of anemone. But no figures came before his sweeping gaze and he started to close a wide circle that would bring him back to where he'd seen the hidden girl. He saw Juan Consalve and six of his crew near the spot, searching with their heads lowered. The captain pointed to places in the rocks. They had picked up tracks, footprints that had been pressed into wet sand and leaves and were still visible. Suddenly, as a hound that had suddenly caught a scent, Consalve moved quickly to the exact spot were the girl lay hidden. Fargo moved the Ovaro forward as the captain bent over, ripped the heavy fronds aside, a lean man with him, and with a triumphant shout, pulled the girl out of her hiding place.

He slapped her in the face, knocked her to the ground, and pulled her to her feet again as Fargo came up. "That's enough," Fargo barked. The captain glared up at him. "Funny way to treat survivors," Fargo said.

"I know what I do." The captain growled. "You can go your way, mister."

"She a prisoner, too?" Fargo asked, edging the horse forward.

"Not for you to worry about. Move on, senhor," the man said. The young woman's eyes met Fargo's and he saw hurt and betrayal in the jet orbs as she shot a quick glance at the captain and the six men with him. All looked back glowering and he took note of the pistols they carried stuck in their belts. All cumbersome, slow-firing European handguns, he noted. None of the men looked as though they'd be fast on the draw, he wagered silently. The advantage would be all his in an opening exchange, Fargo knew, just as he knew exactly what he had to do: send them scattering and give himself the precious seconds he'd need. He didn't want killing if he could avoid it, not with only unanswered questions and more shadow than substance in hand. Drawing a deep breath, he pulled the Colt from the holster at his hip at the same time he sent the Ovaro leaping forward.

He aimed his first shot. The captain clutched his shoulder as he cursed in pain and dropped his hold of the girl. Fargo whirled and fired a volley of shots that had the six crewmen diving for safety. Leaning down, he scooped the girl up into the saddle in front of him. Pressing her head down, he sent the Ovaro racing away, their first shots following. The ground offered no cover and they had enough guns to lay down a solid barrage when they stopped shooting wildly. He sent the Ovaro charging toward the cave as more shots hurtled after him. The horse slipped twice on the still-wet underfooting, but recovered each time, reaching the cave as the next volley of shots fell short. Fargo moved the horse into the cave. He loosened his hold on the girl and she slid from the saddle.

As Fargo dismounted, he could feel the girl's eyes on him but he brushed past her to peer from the mouth of the cave. In the distance, Juan Consalve was gathering more of his crew together as one wrapped a cloth around his shoulder. Fargo felt the girl come alongside him. Still wet, jet black hair clinging to her head, the one-piece dress clinging to her slender body, she nonetheless stood very straight beside him, smallish, high breasts perfect on her shape. "Don't figure you'll understand me but I didn't turn you in back there," Fargo said.

"I know," she said softly in English with hardly the trace of an accent. "That was plain when you took me from them."

"You speak English." He frowned, surprise flooding through him.

"Yes. I am Mei Ling," she said, her voice softly sensuous.

"Fargo. Skye Fargo," he said, still wrestling with his surprise.

Mei Ling's eyes went to Consalve and the others. "What will they do?" she asked.

"Attack, sooner or later," Fargo said. A shiver coursed

through her slender form. He took a blanket from his saddlebag. "Take those wet clothes off," he said and stepped to the edge of the cave. Mei Ling came beside him moments later, almost lost in the blanket wrapped around her. He took the wet dress and spread it on a stone in the sun just outside the cave. "It ought to dry out in an hour," he said.

"Will they wait?" she asked.

"They're in no hurry. They figure all they have to do is come get us or wait for us to try and run," Fargo said.

"Are they right?" she asked.

"I don't figure to let them be," he said, lowering himself to the floor of the cave. She followed, sitting beside him with the blanket demurely wrapped around her. "You've a lot of questions to answer," Fargo said brusquely. "You were on the ship, I take it." She nodded. "How'd you live through the wreck?" he queried.

"The crew left the ship before it hit the rocks. The captain had me taken along. When the lifeboat made it between the rocks, I was on it. But I saw a chance and ran away onshore," Mei Ling said. "That's where you found me hiding."

"Suppose you start from the beginning, tell me everything."

"Everything?"

"About the captain, the ship, about you," Fargo said. "Start with where you learned English."

"In Peking, in a special school for languages. My father is a silk merchant in Peking. I was well-educated," she said.

"What were you doing sailing on a Portuguese trader?" Fargo asked.

"Coming here to America. Over two hundred of us," Mei Ling said. "Only they turned us into prisoners, all of us."

Fargo frowned at her. He wanted to question her more but his keen ears heard the sound from outside. He turned and saw two of the crewmen creeping forward, one on each side of the approach to the cave. "You can tell me the rest later," he said. "We've some visitors that need discouraging."

2

The men crawled up both sides of the slope on their bellies, amateurs that noisily dislodged pebbles every few feet. Fargo drew the big Colt and lay down on his stomach at the edge of the cave. Mei Ling drew back as he motioned to her and he drew a bead on the figure at the right. He fired and the man screamed in pain. Half turning, he rolled down to finally stop halfway down the slope to lie unmoving. The other man was already flinging himself down the other side of the slope, scrambling, sliding, rolling in fear. Fargo holstered the Colt, drew back into the cave, and sat down beside the young woman.

"That was simple enough. They'll stay in place for now, thinking over their options," Fargo said.

"Do they have many?" Mei Ling asked.

"No, but they'll take a while to realize that," he said. "Now let's get on with the rest of your story. You all shipped on with Captain Consalve."

"Paid him a lot of money. Most everyone had papers in order, stamped by the Chinese government. Most were single men, a few families," she said.

"Why were you coming to America?" Fargo interrupted.

"There are not many opportunities for young women in China. Knowing English, I felt I could get a good job here in America," Mei Ling answered. "Consalve advertised for passengers to America. I was one of those who answered. We boarded and the ship set sail. When we were beyond sight of shore, we suddenly changed from passengers to prisoners. At gunpoint, they took everyone's papers, threw them into the sea, and shackled us below deck. He admitted we were going to be sold as slave labor in America. I never felt so helpless in my life. He kept saying he knew just where I'd bring a fancy price."

"I don't have to guess hard at that," Fargo said, taking in the beautiful delicacy of the young woman's features. She'd be an exotic blossom in any whorehouse. "If the captain had honorably fulfilled his bargain, where were you figuring to go when you reached America?" he questioned.

"We were to land at a place called Newport and be met there by Mr. Han. He is head of a colony called Han Village. It is a place where Chinese immigrants can live while they get jobs. Mr. Han helps new immigrants find work. He had become a legend in parts of China through letters sent back home."

"That how you heard about him?"

"Yes. Han Village is near a place called Blue River. Could you get me there?" she asked.

"I can try. But there's a little matter of getting out of here alive, first," Fargo said. Mei Ling's face grew sober and she walked to the mouth of the cave with him. Fargo stared down to the bottom of the slope. The captain and his crew were barely visible behind the line of low rocks. "They'll wait for night to come at us again," he said.

"What can we do? Run for it?" Mei Ling asked.

"That could be risky. I'll work on it. Meanwhile, we get a little sleep. I'm sure you could use it," Fargo said.

"Yes. I've not slept for almost two nights now," she said. He reached out, felt the dress, and pulled it in to her.

"It's dry. You can put it on," he said. She took the dress and somehow managed to slip it on while keeping the blanket around her. Then she stood up and spread the blanket out to lie down on it. He watched her stretch out, her slenderness not without sensuousness, her face delicately etched, lips beautifully formed, her small nose somehow allowing a slight flare to her nostrils. She was really quite beautiful, he decided, combining a young girl's delicacy with a very womanly strength. He lay back nearby, closed his eyes, and catnapped until the dusk began to slide into the cave.

He rose, went to the cave entrance, and peered out at the fast-gathering night. Mei Ling woke, folded the blanket, and put it in the saddlebag. She came beside him as his eyes swept the slope. He had thought of racing out of the cave on the Ovaro when night fell but had discarded the thought. The slope was too treacherous for the horse to take at a gallop and they'd have to be at a gallop to escape the shots that would be sent at them. Eyes narrowed, he saw that it would be dark in minutes. By now, the captain had realized he had only one option. He'd have to reach the mouth of the cave with his crew and send in a barrage of shots, raking the cave from side to side as they advanced.

He'd be firing into the dark, he realized, but he was counting on the fact that with a heavy enough barrage he had to hit his targets. His thinking was all too right, Fargo agreed. If his targets were there waiting to return fire from inside the cave. "Take the horse and go back as far as you can into the cave," he told Mei Ling as he pulled the big sixteen-shot Henry from its saddle case. Dropping onto his stomach, he crawled from the cave in the new darkness and made his way to the far side of the entrance and hunkered down behind a low, almost flat rock. He waited patiently, the rifle to his shoulder, his eyes narrowed as they swept the slope. A new moon emerged to cast a faint light and it wasn't long before Fargo picked out the figures moving up the slope toward the cave.

They were spread out, the uniformed figure of the captain in the center. No crawling this time, they moved in quick, darting motions that brought them to the mouth of the cave in a ragged line where they crouched. With quick, sharp motions, Consalve motioned two of his men to adjust their positions so they could lay down the most effective barrage. As the captain raised his arm to signal the first volley, Fargo's finger tightened on the trigger. Juan Consalve never got to bring his arm down as the heavy .44-caliber shell smashed into him. His arm stiffened and stayed upraised as he half turned and twisted. He did a macabre little dance before toppling to the ground.

But Fargo was already firing more shots, the Henry barking out in rapid-fire succession. Three of the men to the captain's right rose, then fell, hitting the ground at the same time. Another three whirled, peering into the night as they tried to find their attacker. Fargo's shots cut them down before they got off more than two wild shots. Another two came up, firing wildly in Fargo's general direction until Fargo's cool, calm fire cut them down and they pitched backward to roll lifelessly down the slope. Fargo glimpsed a last, lone figure running, half leaping, half rolling over rocks, fleeing in abject fear. Fargo sent a shot after him but the man slipped and fell at the same moment and the shot missed. Listening, Fargo heard him reach the bottom of the slope and keep running. He wouldn't stop, Fargo felt certain, and he waited, letting his eyes scan the ground in front of him. Nothing moved and he pushed to his feet.

"It's over," he called into the cave. "Come on out."

Mei Ling appeared moments after, leading the Ovaro. She halted before him, her black eyes searching his. "It's over because it never happened, thanks to you, Fargo," she said.

"It's called getting the jump on your opponent," he said.

"It's called being someone very special," Mei Ling said unsmilingly, watching as he put the rifle into its case and swung up onto the horse. He reached down and pulled her up to sit in the saddle in front of him. Her slenderness leaned back against him and he was surprised at the soft curvaceousness of her as he sent the Ovaro down the slope.

"They had five prisoners. They're probably tied together at the bottom of the slope someplace. You call out when we reach bottom," he told her as he walked the pinto downward. When they came to the flatland at the base of the slope, Mei Ling began calling out in Chinese.

It only took moments until an answer came and the five figures appeared, tied together as they came forward. Fargo dismounted and cut them loose with his throwing knife while Mei Ling spoke to them. He heard the excitement in their voices as they answered.

"They thank you," Mei Ling said to Fargo. "They are the only survivors. They want to know if we can take them with us."

"Don't see we have a choice." Fargo smiled at her. "Tell them to follow us." She translated his words and climbed into the saddle with him as he moved the horse at a walk, heading east and inland. If she were right about the location of Han Village being in the Blue River area, it wouldn't take him too far from his own destination. He'd almost forgotten about that, he reminded himself, the letter in his jacket pocket recalling the reasons that had brought him to Oregon, a brand-new state wallowing in age-old problems. He pushed the letter aside in his mind and continued to ride till the moon was in the midnight sky, and found himself in country thick with white alder and lodgepole pine. He found a spot to camp and saw the five men lie down off to the side under the alders.

Using his blanket again, Mei Ling lay down beside him in an arbor. She watched him set out his bedroll and undress to his underwear. Her eyes followed him, moving slowly over his muscled body. "There are many things I will say to you, Fargo, but not now," she said.

"Good. It's time for sleep, not talk," Fargo said, and closing his eyes for emphasis, he let sleep come to him until the new day dawned. He was the first to wake, and he quickly dressed and surveyed the terrain. He saw sugar pine and western juniper besides the other trees he'd noted during the night. A half-dozen black-tailed deer crossed in front of him and he spotted a short-tailed weasel. He found a stand of wild plums for breakfast and by the time the new sun flooded the land, Mei Ling was in the saddle with him. He held the horse to a walk and the five men stayed close at his heels. The soft curviness of Mei Ling hadn't changed any, he noted, still surprised as she pressed back against his groin in the saddle. He threaded his way through rolling hills well timbered with buckthorns, black cottonwoods, Rocky Mountain maple, and juniper. A narrow trail suddenly widened with a thick stand of cottonwoods on both sides. Four riders appeared, coming toward him, and Fargo reined to a halt.

His instincts rose in instant warning as the men stopped in front of him. Long ago, Fargo had learned that men could be read perhaps more easily than trails. Their faces, their eyes, their body language, their very clothes, left prints as real as leaves, brush, grass or soil. These four were trouble. It was in the covetous way the first one looked at Mei Ling and it was in their faces, hard and cruel-mouthed, faces of bitter men with bitter souls. His eyes took in gunbelts of cracked leather and holsters too worn to hang tight. Drifters with little else but avarice to their names, Fargo thought. The first one tore his eyes from Mei Ling, a worn Stetson covering a sharp, hollow-cheeked face, and glanced at the five Chinese men who'd halted behind the Ovaro. "What've we got ourselves here?" he asked, a sneer in his voice.

"Travelers," Fargo said mildly and felt Mei Ling's body stiffen. She had her own quick instincts.

"Travelers?" the hollow-cheeked one echoed. "Looks more like you got yourself some goods for sale, mister."

"Nothing's for sale here," Fargo said evenly and took in the four men with another quick glance. He was fast enough to take all four, he decided. Their loose-hanging holsters were an added certainty but there were still four of them. One might be fairly fast. He wanted an added edge and there was nothing better than nervousness.

"How much for her?" the hollow-cheeked one asked, nodding to Mei Ling.

"You have hearing problems?" Fargo asked mildly. "I told you nothing's for sale here."

"You got counting problems, mister?" the man said, his voice hardening. "There are four of us."

"I can count real well," Fargo said, keeping his voice mild.

"I guess we'll just have to help ourselves," the man said.

"That's a bad idea," Fargo said calmly and saw the man's forehead furrow as he stared back. The first flare of apprehension had pushed up inside him. Fargo's eyes stayed unmoving.

"Bluffing's a fast way to get yourself killed," the man said a little too loudly.

Fargo smiled. "So's making a bad call," he said. The man exchanged quick glances with the others. They blinked back, nervousness flashing in their eyes. Like most bullies and braggarts, they were aware of the hollowness inside their masks. But they had to borrow strength from each other, Fargo realized, and kept the smile on his face.

"You're asking for it, mister," the one growled.

"I'm letting the little lady down. Neither of us want her taking a stray bullet," Fargo said.

"No, we don't want that," the man agreed and Fargo met Mei Ling's quick glance, fear in her black orbs. He nodded to her and helped her swing from the saddle onto the other side of the Ovaro. Her feet had just touched the ground when Fargo saw the hollow-cheeked one reach for his gun. The others went to their holsters, too, but their draws were all jerky, nervousness making them yank at their weapons. Fargo's Colt left its holster in one smooth, lightninglike motion. His first shot blasted the hollow-cheeked man out of his saddle. The man hadn't hit the ground when Fargo's next two shots, so fast they sounded almost as one, sent the next two men toppling sideways from their horses. The fourth one had his gun out, almost raised to fire when Fargo's shot shattered his right forearm. Cursing in pain, he doubled up in the saddle as the pistol fell to the ground, pressing his arm to his side.

Fargo dismounted, approached the last one, and kicked the gun into the brush. "Hit the ground," he snapped and the man swung from the horse, pain wreathing his face. He waited, bent over, fear joining the pain in his face.

"Don't kill me, mister. I had to go along with Harry," he whined.

"You're not worth killing," Fargo said. "You work for somebody?"

"No," the man said.

"Small-time freelancers," Fargo said, contempt in his voice. "Start walking," he ordered and the man began to hurry away, still clutching his arm to his side. When he was out of sight Fargo turned to Mei Ling and nodded to the five Chinese men. "Tell them to use the horses," he said. She translated his words and the five men climbed onto the horses, two doubling up. They were no horsemen, he saw, as they clung to the saddle horns almost in desperation. But Fargo was able to put the Ovaro into a slow trot and make better time. As he rode, the incident stayed with him. It had been more than an ugly and dangerous moment. It said something more. The four men had just assumed he was trafficking in slave labor and that meant but one thing. The trade in Chinese slave labor was a widespread fact of life in the new state of Oregon. The thought lay inside him, disturbing him more ways than he could immediately define. It certainly explained Captain Consalve and his ill-fated trip.

He'd not share his thoughts with Mei Ling, he decided, and took a narrow path down a small hillside, riding onto level ground covered with Spanish clover. He saw a man driving a dry-goods wagon with the typical paneled body and outswept sides. He reined up when he reached the wagon, drawing a nod from the driver. "Han Village," he said.

The man took in Mei Ling and the others. "Keep going northeast. You'll come to it," he said.

"Obliged," Fargo returned and sent the pinto on, the strange little procession following. Mei Ling rode in silence. He estimated they had gone almost twenty miles, the day starting to slide toward an end, when the village came into sight. It spread over a much larger area than he'd expected, part of it on flat land, part on two low hills. He took in a number of houses, most made of wood but some of stone, and more than a few were hard-packed mud houses. A number had thatched roofs, he noted, and he saw two structures that resembled barracks. Men and women in traditional Chinese clothes dotted the village and as he walked the pinto forward he saw others tending to small fields of barley, lettuce, squash, and potatoes. They also raised wild rice off to the far side of the village.

Two well-built young Chinese men came toward Fargo as he reined to a halt. Close behind them was an elderly man with gray hair, a gray, wispy goatee, and crinkles around his narrow eyes. His face, surprisingly youthful despite the crinkles and gray hair, held both strength and kindness. He wore a dark blue brocade jacket, three-quarter length, buttoned down the front, very Oriental in cut, with loose-fitting, blue trousers. Fargo saw his eyes move over the five men that followed and paused on Mei Ling, who slid to the ground.

"Nǐ hǎo," the elderly figure said to Mei Ling.

"Nǐ hǎo," she answered with a bow.

"Nide jiào shénme mingzi?"

"Mei Ling," she replied. *"Nǐ ne?"*

"Han," the elderly man said and Mei Ling spoke quickly and he answered, their conversation going on until she turned to Fargo.

"I told Elder Han about Captain Consalve, the storm, and all you've done, Fargo," she said. "He thanks you for everyone here in his village."

Han's eyes stayed on Fargo. "I have much to say but my English is not very good," he said with a pronounced Chinese accent. "I will speak through Mei Ling. It will

33

be better." Fargo nodded and Mei Ling began to translate as Han spoke.

"Han says there is much trouble here. My people work hard for an honest wage. There are good people who employ the Chinese immigrants who have come here. They come to me and I supply them with the good workers they need. But there are many who capture honest people from my village. So many of our young men, and women, have just disappeared. Then there are others who bring in shiploads of young men for slave labor, such as your Captain Consalve." Mei Ling halted as Han paused, took a deep breath, and spoke again. "It has come to me that there are more who plan to bring in more slave labor. I feel helpless and frightened."

"Ask him about the nearest town and the sheriff," Fargo said.

After a moment's exchange with Han, Mei Ling answered. "The town nearest in the Blue River area is Badger Hollow. The sheriff has authority but no power. He is alone and afraid. His name is Ed Yancey."

"Does he know the names of the men who plan to bring in more slave labor?" Fargo queried.

"No," Mei Ling said after an exchange with Han. "He has heard only talk and rumor. The only reality is the young men who are abducted. Han asks if you can help us."

Fargo glanced up. Dusk was sliding quickly over the village, almost as an omen of a curtain coming down. He turned his hands up helplessly. "I've a job to do. It's what brought me here. I've got to go on," he said. "To help you would take a lot of time, a lot of searching, and a lot of luck. I haven't enough of any of those things and I have to honor my own commitments."

Mei Ling finished translating and Han nodded. In his face, Fargo saw acceptance and understanding, qualities out of another culture and another wisdom. Mei Ling listened to the gray-goateed, elderly figure and turned to Fargo. "He understands and is grateful for what you have done. I will show you a place to spend the night, kept for unexpected visitors," she said and as night fell he followed her and a young Chinese boy. The boy led the way to a round, thatched-roof structure fashioned of wood and packed mud. A candle burned inside and the boy hurried away. "I will come back," Mei Ling said and walked away, her slender shape quickly disappearing into the night.

Fargo unsaddled the Ovaro and saw a communal fire lighted in the center of the village, figures gathering around it. He brought his things into the hut, took off his jacket, and examined the cot against one side of the house. A large wooden basin filled with water stood beside it and a curtain cut off part of the single room. Peering behind it, he saw a primitive toilet with towels atop a small table. He returned to the main part of the room, sat down on the cot, and stretched out. He'd only relaxed a few minutes when Mei Ling appeared carrying a metal dish, with two clay plates. Inside the big, saucerlike dish, steam rose up from a combination of cut vegetables and meat, everything smelling delicious. "Rabbit and assorted vegetables," Mei Ling said, sitting down beside him, handing him a plate and a pair of chopsticks.

"Afraid I've never used these," Fargo told her.

"Not to be concerned," she said and proceeded to

show him how to use the wooden utensils. She was a quick and good teacher, and he found himself handling the chopsticks with an efficiency that surprised him. The meal was tasty and Mei Ling set the plates aside when they finished. She faced him, her jet eyes searching his face. "I am yours," she said simply. "After what you have done for me there is nothing else I can give you. I have nothing else."

"You don't need to give me anything," Fargo said.

"You saved my life. That is deserving of a special gift. It is our custom. I have no other gift to give," she said.

"It's against my principles to turn down a free drink or a willing woman but once in a while I make an exception," Fargo said.

She rose, stood very straight in front of him, smallish, high breasts thrusting forth insouciantly, her body willow-wand sinuousness. "I do not please you?" she said.

"You please me very much. That's why I won't settle for thanks. I don't expect I can explain that to you," he said.

"I understand. I will wait till you come back. Then maybe you will understand," she said.

He smiled. "What makes you so sure I'll come back?"

"Because you have a *ch'i* of goodness, Fargo," Mei Ling said.

"A *ch'i*?" He frowned. "You want to explain that?"

"*Ch'i* is a word of many meanings. It has been used by all the ancient scholars, from Confucius, Mencius, Lao Tzu, the Logicians, the Taoists, the Mystics, all of them, yet it is hard to explain. There can be a *ch'i* of anger and a *ch'i* of pleasure, a *ch'i* of order and of disorder. Perhaps a *ch'i* can best be described as an inner force, that quality that makes a thing what it is. Your *ch'i* is that of goodness," Mei Ling said.

"There'd be plenty who'd disagree with that," Fargo said wryly.

"They do not know you."

"Hell, you don't know me. We've just about met," Fargo said.

"Knowing someone is an inner thing, not an outer one," she said with calm finality and he found himself admiring something more than her quiet loveliness.

"Then I guess I'll be coming back when I'm finished," he said.

"And I will wait for you," she said. She stepped forward and her lips brushed his cheek and she was gone, silently as a firefly vanishes. He undressed in the little house and slept soundly till morning came. When he rose, he washed with the basin behind the curtain. He was halfway dressed when he heard the faint sound outside. Hurriedly finishing, he pushed the curtain aside to find a clay cup of tea waiting. It was smoky in flavor and bracing and he went outside when he finished. The village was quiet, figures working in the vegetable fields on the hillsides, a calm, ordered air to the scene.

He saw neither Han nor Mei Ling, saddled the Ovaro, and rode from the village and realized he felt sorry he couldn't stay to help them. Plainly, there were dark forces on the loose in this new state of Oregon, forces that belied the bright sunlit fields of wild roses, mountain mahoganies and shadscale. He rode north, and came to Badger Hollow first, a town with little to recommend it. Riding slowly through it, he saw worn clapboard buildings, a few stores, a wheelwright's shop and the saloon, the largest building in the town. Two stories high, the second story fronted small windows where he saw a number of young women drying clothes and lounging idly. Heavy, four-wheel logging trucks with extra-wide tires dotted the streets, along with a handful of Owensboro California rack-bed wagons.

He saw the sheriff's office and caught a glimpse of a middle-aged man with sand-colored hair and a slight paunch. He rode out of Badger Hollow, certain he'd be visiting the town again. Following the instructions he'd been sent, he continued north through land of low, rolling hills, well-timbered with madrone, dwarf maple, buckthorn, and mountain ash. The tree cover grew thicker as he proceeded further north and it was mid-morning when he came upon a cleared piece of land where what seemed to be a ranch rose up before him. He took in a stone main house, corrals, bunkhouses, and ranch hands lounging alongside them, a covered well, and three large barns. Beside the barns he noted three big mountain wagons with oversized brakes, one filled with carpenter's tools, axes, awls, hammers, nail boxes, mallets, and levels, the other two holding various lengths of lumber.

Only one thing was missing from the picture. There were no steers, hogs, sheep, or mustangs, only a dozen stray chickens strutting across the front yard. But the large initials in wood over the main house, A-M-F, told him he was in the right place. He reined up outside the main house and as he dismounted, the door opened and a young woman came outside wearing a tan shirt and a brown skirt. His eyes held on hazel hair and hazel eyes to match, an even-featured face with a straight nose and full lips, the hazel hair brushed back and worn loosely. Deep, full breasts filled out the tan shirt and a long waist fitted her tall figure. She regarded him with a faint smile that held just an edge of arrogance in it. "Sky Fargo," she said.

"Good guess," he answered.

"No guess. Ben Denton told me about that Ovaro of yours," she said. He nodded. Ben Denton had been the reference in the note he'd been sent. An old friend, Fargo had broken many a trail for him, he remembered.

"Mr. Foster sent for me. Is he around?" Fargo asked.

"No. He died in April," the young woman said, the faint smile staying on her lips.

Fargo's mind leaped backward and he felt his brows lift. "The letter he sent me was dated June," he said.

"I know. I sent it," she said.

"And signed his name?"

"Look at the signature again," she said, amusement in her hazel eyes. He fished the letter from his pocket and read the signature.

"A. M. Foster," he said.

"That's me, Alberta Marilyn Foster. My father was Albert Madison Foster," she said.

His eyes narrowed at her. "I don't figure being tricked is the right way to start a job," he said. "Maybe you'd better explain some more. Straight talk this time."

"Please come inside," Alberta Foster said and he followed her into the house, his irritation tempered by watching the way her hips swung to let the brown skirt fall over a full, round rear.

3

Fargo found himself inside a large living room in the house, very well furnished with sofas, deep chairs, rugs, and drapes. Alberta Marilyn Foster turned, faced him, and flashed a smile that took the edge of arrogance from her face, replacing it with a new attractiveness. "I wasn't sure you'd come if I'd signed the letter," she said. "A lot of men don't like working for a woman. You know that."

He nodded, conceding her point and letting his glance go out of the window where the hands lounged by the bunkhouses. "Seems you've overcome that," he said.

"Many of them worked for my father. They're used to me and I pay them top dollar," she said, lowering herself onto a sofa. "Please sit down." She gestured and he sank down beside her, watching her deep breasts sway as she half turned. She had looks, money, and power, plus a very definite sensuality to her. She was well aware of her weapons, he decided. "I sent for you because I heard you were the very best and I have a special job for you," she said, stretching her arms to rest atop the back of the sofa, her breasts pressing tight against the tan shirt. "I want you to break a different kind of trail for me, Fargo. Three trails, in fact."

He smiled. "You're paying enough for three trails," he said.

"One trail will go from here to the coastline, to the sea itself. A second will go from here northeast, the third from here southeast. Three trails that will form a Y lying down, what cattlemen would call a lazy Y."

"One to the coastline," he repeated. "How far do you want the other two to go?"

"You can stop when you've reached fifty miles, give or take a few miles," Alberta said somewhat airily.

"Stop where?" Fargo pressed.

"Wherever," she said.

"Sounds like you want a trail to nowhere." Fargo frowned.

"New towns will be started where each trail ends. I've some backers who've guaranteed that," she said.

"A town usually comes first. If it gets big enough or is in a good place, a trail follows as folks go to it," Fargo said.

"I'm reversing the usual way of things," Alberta Foster said.

"Is this what you meant by a different kind of trail?" Fargo asked.

"No. You won't need to find a trail five hundred steers can travel. I don't want a trail to move big herds," she said.

"Why not?"

"Because I won't be moving cattle. I'm establishing a stagecoach run. I expect I'll have three stages in time."

"You figure folks will take a stage to towns just built?" he questioned.

"Not your ordinary travelers. You've heard of tourists, haven't you?" she asked and he nodded. "I expect there'll be a lot of tourists come to see the new state of Oregon, to look hard and decide if they want to settle down here. My stagecoaches will help them do that. Naturally, I don't want competition. That's why I want you to break trails only wide enough for a Concord or single wagon. I don't want trails any cattle herder can use and widen. That's what I'm paying you fancy money to find for me," she said.

"I'll do my best," he said.

Her hand closed over his. "That's all I want," she said. "I'll need maps, Fargo. You ever make maps?"

"I have," he said.

"Good. I'll want a map of each trail with all the main markers set down clearly. I've paper and a plug-stoppered ink bottle for you," she said.

"There's one thing. I find a trail, that doesn't mean a stage can just roll over it. A trail could need clearing in places, smoothing in others, cutting back timbers in still others."

"I know that. Once you've mapped a trail, I'll have a crew smooth out every spot you mark. When I'm through, the trail will be ready for any stage," she said, pushing to her feet quickly. "Let me get a drink to celebrate."

"Little premature, isn't it?" he queried.

"No, I've complete confidence you'll bring me the trails I want," she said, disappearing into an adjoining room. She returned with two glasses of rye whiskey, then sat down beside him again. She had embarked on a damn strange venture, he reflected as he sipped the whiskey beside her. Her enthusiasm and air of assurance made it all seem reasonable when it was far from that, starting with her initial premise of tourists. But her attractiveness and sincerity made one want to believe in her. Besides, for what she was paying, she deserved believing. He'd table his usual cynicism, he told himself.

He finished the drink and rose. "I'll be getting on. You've set out a damn formidable job, Alberta," he said. She rose, went into the next room, and returned with a small leather pouch.

"Paper and pen for your map making," she said, and linking her arm in his, she walked outside to the Ovaro with him.

"I see corrals and barns but I don't see any livestock," he commented.

"Father had cattle. Hogs, too, but I got rid of all that. A stage line will be much more profitable," Alberta said. As she walked with him, he felt the soft side of one breast press against his arm and shot a glance at her. She had to be aware of her touch against him but she gave no sign of it. When they reached the pinto she turned to him, the hazel eyes holding little lights of private amusement in them. "You find those trails for me and there'll be a bonus in it," she said.

"You're paying good dollar," he said.

"There are all kinds of bonuses," Alberta said. He smiled as he swung onto the horse. This strange job would certainly be a new challenge but it might bring old pleasures, he decided with a last glance at the tall, deep-breasted attractiveness of her. He sent the Ovaro forward as she turned and strode into the house, the late-day sun glinting on her hazel hair. Alberta Marilyn Foster was an uncommonly attractive woman, he decided, despite her embrace of tenuous ventures.

Fargo rode at a slow trot as the day neared an end. He'd begin with finding a trail to the coast. That would form the base of the lazy Y. Riding until night descended, he quickly realized that no easy task lay ahead. Small hills comprised most of the terrain, crowding each other and each covered with thick growths of western juniper, red alder, Sitka spruce, and mountain ash. The low growth was mostly chaparral and the thickets of yellow bitter-brush blossoms. Before night fell he decided he'd find very few places that even resembled a plateau and few flat passages. He bedded down under the towering trunk of a Sitka spruce and slept quickly, waking twice during the night to the sound of bears foraging nearby. He was in the saddle again with the new day, riding west as he noted that the crowded hills didn't grow any friendlier.

After exploring every cut, every passage, and every green-swathed trail that offered itself, it was nearly noon when he realized he had swung northwest. Correcting his direction, he suddenly came upon the first passage that held any promise. It ran down along the bottom of one set of hills, curved around a pair of twisted junipers, and later a tall slab of granite. He halted, took the ink and paper from the pouch, and began to draw a map, noting each of the markers. By midafternoon he was beginning to feel encouraged. He'd explored further, followed the signs left by black-tailed deer and an occasional elk, and had the beginnings of a good map set down on the paper. He finished drawing another marker where a very tall Sitka spruce rose apart from other trees and fronted a sudden curve.

Putting the pouch away, he came across a road that

crossed the one he'd been exploring and unexpectedly leveled off. The road was one fairly well traveled, he saw, with wheel prints as well as hoof marks, and ran north to south. He left his trail and turned onto it out of curiosity more than anything else. Rounding a curve, he pulled to a halt, shock and disgust swirling through him. The lone figure hung from the branch of a cottonwood at the side of the road, turning slowly, the head twisted to one side where the rope encircled the neck. Fargo leapt from the saddle and ran to the figure. It was a slender young Chinese man in a torn shirt and loose black trousers. Fargo reached one hand up to the man's mouth to see if he could detect breathing.

"Don't bother. He's dead," a voice said and Fargo spun, the Colt in his hand at once. His lake blue eyes blazed at a smallish man with straying wisps of gray hair, a tattered leather vest, and worn jeans. A grizzled face made of lines and crinkles stared back at him from beneath a battered derby hat.

"Easy, friend," the grizzled face said and Fargo's eyes flicked to the horse behind the man and the pack mule beside it, burdened with shovels, axes, leather bags, and pots and pans. "Just got here a few minutes before you," the man said. "Checked him out right away."

Fargo let the Colt drop back into its holster. "You know him?" he questioned.

"Nope. Just came onto him the way you did. I was taking the road back to my place," the man said.

Fargo glanced at the hanging figure and touched the man's face again, this time with the back of his hand. "He hasn't been hanging here long. He's still warm," Fargo said.

"They hung him here as an example. That's what they do. This road's well traveled," the grizzled face said.

"An example?" Fargo asked.

"To anyone else thinking of running away," the man said.

"Who's *they*?" Fargo asked.

The man's face grew more crinkled as he shrugged. "Could be any of them using Chinese slave labor," he said.

Fargo, his mouth a tight line, drew the double-edged blade from his calf holster and cut the rope from around the man's neck, catching the lifeless form in his arms and lowering it to the ground. "No more example," he said bitterly and pulled the figure into the trees. Putting the knife away, he let his eyes sweep the roadway, and quickly found what he sought, hoofprints of horses held in a tight knot. "Four to six of them," he said, kneeling down. His hands touched the edges of the hoofprints, fingertips read the soil as other men read a newspaper. They took in the feel of firmness, the contours of shape and depth, the touch of warmth and smoothness. "Their prints aren't more than ten minutes old," he murmured.

The grizzled face showed surprise. "You some sort of scout, mister?" the old man asked.

"Some folks call me the Trailsman," Fargo said as he stood up and pulled himself onto the Ovaro. In his mind flashed the vision of the Portuguese trader and its human cargo and the fine-featured, proud face of Mei Ling. He felt the anger spiral through him. "I'm going to set an example of my own," he said.

"You expect to find them?"

"I'll find them. One has a bad chip on his horse's right forefoot," Fargo said.

"Mind if I tag along?" the man asked.

Fargo eyed the mule. "I won't be hanging back for you," he said.

"Don't expect that," the grizzled figure said. He was pulling himself onto his horse, not without effort, Fargo noted, as he sent the pinto into a fast canter. Picking up the riders was easy enough. They rode bunched together and left a clear trail. The road stayed well-traveled, Fargo saw, with numerous prints of individual riders and wagon wheel tracks. The knot of horsemen soon came into sight, riding slowly and casually. Fargo leaned from the saddle, scanned the hoofprints to be sure he was right, and found the chipped shoe print. His jaw tightening, he sent the Ovaro into the cottonwoods at the side of the road. He passed the riders and returned to the road in front of them, blocking their path. They reined to a halt and Fargo moved the Ovaro to the side so he had the men all in one glance. Five, he noted, and quickly took in the riders, all hard-faced men, but these had well-kept holsters and all carried big six-shot, single-action Remington army revolvers, good, fast shooting weapons.

They frowned collectively at him and one with long black hair pulled back in a ponytail spoke up for the others. "Something we can do for you, mister?" he said.

"Maybe," Fargo answered. "There was a man hanging from a tree back a ways. You boys hang him there?"

"What makes you think that?" the long-haired one asked.

"You were there."

"How do you know that?" The man frowned.

"One of your horses has a chipped shoe," Fargo said.

The man exchanged quick glances. "We were there," the ponytailed one said. "That don't mean we hung him."

"No, it doesn't," Fargo agreed. "You see who did?"

"No. We just stopped by to watch him swing," one of the others sniggered.

"Well, he's not there anymore," Fargo said.

"What's that mean?" the long-haired one snapped.

"I took him down," Fargo said and watched their faces immediately darken.

"What the hell gave you leave to do that?" the long-haired one growled.

"Didn't like seeing him there," Fargo said evenly.

"You're a regular busybody, aren't you, mister?" one of the others said.

"Sometimes," Fargo said.

"Well, now, maybe you'd like to take his place," the long-haired one said.

"Didn't figure to do that," Fargo said but their angry reaction had told him enough. He tightened his forearm. They'd explode quickly, he knew.

"Then you've made your last mistake, mister," the man said. He reached for his gun but Fargo had already anticipated that. The Colt was in his hand in one quick, smooth motion. His shot caught the long-haired one instantly and the man fell forward, his saddle horn suddenly streaked with red. Fargo had already swung the Colt a fraction of an inch, his shot toppling the second man, then the third beside him. But the last two were faster than he'd counted on, both with their Remingtons out and raised. Fargo cursed silently and started to dive from the saddle when the explosion came from behind him, too heavy and too loud to be anything but rifle fire. He felt the shot hurl past his shoulder and saw one of the two remaining riders blown from his horse as if swept away by a giant, invisible hand.

Fargo held the Colt on the last man whose eyes had widened in surprise and sudden fear as he let the Remington fall from his hand. "Smart move," Fargo said, and cast a glance behind him at the grizzled figure on his horse, an old, heavy-firing Hawkens plains rifle in his hands. "Much obliged," Fargo said.

"Just came up in time," the older man said and Fargo moved the Ovaro closer to the fifth man, who waited, fear still in his eyes.

"Why?" Fargo flung at him, certain the single word would suffice.

"We always do that when we catch them. He ran away," the man said with defensiveness.

"From where?"

"Sam Bundy's place," the man said.

"Who's Sam Bundy?" Fargo questioned.

"He owns the Bundy mines," the man said.

"Copper, mostly, some tungsten," the grizzled figure put in from behind Fargo.

"You go back and tell this Sam Bundy if his boys hang another man I'll come after him. The name's Fargo, Skye Fargo. Tell him to remember it," Fargo said. "Now ride."

Swallowing hard, the man left in a fast canter, vanishing down the road. Fargo turned to the grizzled figure. "I owe you, old-timer," he said. "I never did get a name for you."

"Willie Baxter."

"You said you were going to your place. You live around here, then."

"Down a ways." The older man nodded.

"Then you'd know the people and the land," Fargo said.

"I'm a walking history book," Willie Baxter said.

Fargo smiled. "I might just like a lesson," he said. "But first I'm taking this poor devil to be buried by his people."

"To Han Village?"

Fargo's brows lifted. "You know it?"

"Helped them run water pipes to their rice fields," Willie said. "Mind if I go along with you?"

"Come along," Fargo said and led the way back to where the man lay in the cottonwoods.

"Lay him over Jenny," Willie said, gesturing to his mule. "She can carry him. She's strong." Fargo draped the man over the back of the mule and climbed onto the Ovaro. He led the way at a walk, down the road, and following Willie's directions to a shortcut, reached the village. Figures quickly gathered as the strange little procession entered the village and Fargo saw Han hurrying to him, Mei Ling a few steps behind. She wore a silk dress that clung to her willow-wand figure, highlighting every slender line of it. Others came to help lift the man's body from the mule, and lay it gently on the ground.

"That is Tzu Sung," Han said as Mei Ling translated. "He disappeared two months ago, never returned from his job one day. I was certain he'd been seized and forced into slave labor, like so many others have."

"We will take care of him," Mei Ling said and the lifeless figure was gently carried away, Han accompanying the others as they left. Mei Ling stayed with Fargo, her eyes searching his face. "Have you come to stay and help us? Is your job finished?" she asked.

"Just started," he said. "How are you doing?"

"Good. Han found work for me with a man named Ryan who makes shirts. I was hired to help manage and translate for him. He uses a number of Chinese workers," Mei Ling said. "I'd hoped you had come to stay," she added.

"Sorry. But after what I've seen I decided I'll be stopping by to look in on you more often," Fargo said.

"I should like that," she said, her smile somehow both bold and shy. He waved to her as he swung onto the pinto and she hurried away, every part of her slender figure moving as one. Willie Baxter came alongside him as he rode from the village and gestured to the sun touching the horizon.

"It'll be night soon. Got a place to stay?" he asked.

"I'll bed down somewhere," Fargo said.

"You're welcome at my place. I've extra room," Willie said.

"Thanks. I've some questions you might answer," Fargo said as Willie Baxter led the way down a narrow trail, which was hardly more than a deer path, and emerged where the terrain widened. The house appeared not long afterward, really a long, double cabin set down beneath two towering Sitka spruce. A sturdy, covered lean-to adjoined the structure, large enough for both horses and the mule. As Fargo unsaddled the Ovaro, Willie Baxter went into the house and when Fargo followed he found himself in a spacious room with chairs, a stone fireplace, and a stove with hooked rugs on the floor. The second part of the cabin lay beyond a heavy curtain used as a divider.

"You build this place yourself?" Fargo queried.

Willie shook his head. "Inherited from a old friend years ago," he said and removed the black, battered derby to reveal thinning gray hair. "Got some good rabbit stew simmering," he said and Fargo drew in the aroma as Willie stirred a big, black iron kettle. "The other room's yours," he said as he went outside to put away his horse and mule. Fargo took his things into the adjoining room, unpacked some and returned to give the kettle another stir as Willie came back and night descended. Bringing out a bottle of rye and two glasses, he sat down with Fargo. "How'd you get to know the Chinese girl?" he asked. "She likes you. It was in her eyes."

"She's grateful," Fargo said and recounted the story of the wreck and the Portuguese slave trader.

"She should be grateful but it's more than that," Willie said.

"You an expert on women among your other trades?" Fargo laughed.

"Dealt with enough in my years. But it's the Chinese I'm talking about. They respect someone who has a quality they call *yi*, which they call human-heartedness. Learned that dealing with them over the years."

"*Yi* . . . human-heartedness," Fargo echoed, turning the phrase in his mind.

"We might call it righteousness but I like their way of putting it better," Willie said.

"I'm bothered by what I've seen here," Fargo said.

"The traffic in Chinese slave labor? It's getting worse. It's the bad taking advantage of the good, the strong taking advantage of the weak. There's nothing new in that."

"That doesn't mean it has to go on," Fargo said.

Willie screwed up his face into more crinkles. "It's made to go on, friend. The sheep keep coming. The wolves are waiting. That's just being realistic."

"There's being realistic and there's giving up," Fargo said.

Willie cocked his head to one side as he regarded the big man in front of him. "You've some of the crusader in you, Fargo," he said.

"I wouldn't call it anything that fancy. I just believe in helping those who need help and I don't like hanging and kidnapping," Fargo said. "Tell me what you can about the way of things here."

"The Chinese come with hopes, pay their way here. Some folks pay them an honest wage for an honest day's work. They're good, hard workers. But there are the others, the wolves. They know a good thing when they see it. They're the ones who arrange to bring over slave labor, make deals with the likes of that Portuguese captain. They bring in the slave labor and if they run short they snatch up those working here."

"Like Sam Bundy?"

"He's one. There are two more big users of slave labor, the Greavey brothers, who run a logging operation, and the Gallarde family. They run a big vegetable and rice farm. Then there's Bart Egan, who has a chain of saloons and cathouses."

"Don't have to guess what he wants his slave labor for," Fargo said. "Chinese girls would bring an extra price tag."

"The trouble is that there are at least ten more outfits that want to expand or start up if they could get labor. Labor's the only thing holding them back. I'd guess they wouldn't turn down slave labor," Willie said.

"Not a nice picture," Fargo muttered.

"This is a fine land with a deep poison running through it, my friend," Willie said. "What's brought you here?"

"Was hired to break a trail, a different kind of trail," Fargo said.

"Seems that'd be more than enough to keep you busy," Willie said.

"It is, but maybe I can do a little more," Fargo said.

"Who wants a trail broken in these parts?" Willie asked.

"A young woman, Alberta Marilyn Foster. Maybe you know the family. She says her pa was a big man around here."

"Oh, he was that, all right," Willie said, his voice taking on an edge.

"You mean something more than that, old-timer," Fargo smiled.

"Guess I do. Albert Madison Foster was a no-good, robbing, stealing son of a bitch. Everything he owned, and there was plenty, he cheated somebody out of or just plain took from them. He had all the ethics of a polecat," Willie said bitterly.

"Sounds like you never cared for him," Fargo said blandly.

"You'll have to look hard to find somebody who did.

But then there aren't that many left alive to tell about him."

"Of course, that doesn't mean his daughter's the same," Fargo said.

"No, it doesn't. I never got to know her. Old man Foster kept her in the background. She's taken over now that he's gone but I can't say anything much more than that about her," Willie said and Fargo caught something unfinished in his voice.

"You've something more to add," he remarked.

Willie Baxter gave a reluctant smile. "You never know how far the apple will fall from the tree," he said and Fargo waited. "Sometimes the child tries hard not to be like the father. Sometimes you can't recognize the father in the child. Then sometimes they're two of a kind. It's hard to figure."

"I'd guess Alberta Foster is her own woman," Fargo said.

"Let's hope so," Willie Baxter said.

"She's about to start a stage line, wants me to find her three trails, one to the coast, one northwest, one southeast."

"To where?"

"No place yet," Fargo smiled. "But she says she has backers who've agreed to build towns. She wants trails only big enough for her stages."

"Sounds plumb crazy to me," Willie said.

"Doesn't do a lot for me, either. But she seems real smart. She might have something. Anyway, I'm not being paid to second-guess her," Fargo said.

"Good luck." Willie sniffed and rose to dish out the stew. The meal was tasty and filling and Fargo turned in soon after. He slept soundly, woke with the new sun, and found Willie up with coffee brewed.

"Thanks for the hospitality, Willie," Fargo said when he retrieved his saddle.

"The place is yours anytime," Willie said. "We might cross paths, anyway. I get around in my travels."

"Hope we will. I might need another history lesson," Fargo said and Willie waved his good-bye when he rode away. He returned to the trail he'd begun and continued to probe, explore, and mark the map as he drew it. The trail twisted and turned as he pursued its path, almost as if in protest at giving up its secrets. But he persisted, working doggedly, using all the trail lore he had amassed in his years. He refused to be sent down false passages and led astray by siren trails. By day's end he was dissatisfied at how little he had done and the next day proved no easier, the terrain determined to hide its treasures. It took him unexpected days to map a trail through terrain that proved deceptively difficult. Finally, under a hot afternoon sun, too many days later, he reached the coast. He could hear the sound of the surf before he saw it.

When he came in sight of the shore he saw a wide beach where long spaces rose up between towering rocks that rose from the sea beyond the shoreline. Each huge rock seemed a monument to a prehistoric era when the world was still forming. He sent the Ovaro across the hard-packed sand of the beach, toward a figure prying mussels from a line of low rocks. "Afternoon," he called out as he reached the man, who wore oilskins against the drenching spray that buffeted him. "I don't know this part of the coast and I'm wondering where I might be," Fargo said.

"You're a little north of Seal Rock," the man said.

Fargo drew the map from its pouch. "Seal Rock," he repeated as he wrote on the map. Finished, his eyes went back to the sea. "This high tide?" he asked and the man nodded. "Then the beach runs out further," Fargo said.

"About five hundred yards," the man said. "Then it drops straight off into deep water."

"Obliged," Fargo said, and turning the pinto, he began retracing his steps. He followed the trail he had broken, rechecked the map, made small changes, and grew satisfied that anyone using the map could follow the trail. Two days later, as the afternoon lengthened, he arrived at the Foster place. The hands were still lounging outside the bunkhouses. Alberta came to the door, her hazel eyes warm with welcome as she brought him into the house.

"Been waiting," she said.

He drew the map from the pouch and handed it to her. "Your trail to the coast," he said.

She gave a squeal of delight and impulsively threw her arms around his neck, clinging long enough and close enough for him to feel the wonderfully soft warmth of her breasts as they pressed against him. She pulled back after a moment and he wanted to think he saw a banked fire glint in the hazel eyes before she concentrated on the map. "Wonderful. I'll get a crew started right away. I see you've marked where trees need cutting back and the trail in general smoothed. This calls for a drink," Alberta said, and leading him to the sofa, she quickly poured drinks. "You going to start on the next one right away?" she asked.

"Definitely," he said and she picked up something in his voice.

"You sound as though you expect problems," she said.

"If it's anything like the last one. This is real tricky terrain. It looks easier than it is to uncover trails," Fargo said.

"That's why I sent for you. I didn't expect the ordinary tracker could do it," Alberta said. She leaned back into the sofa, her arms lifted to rest on the back, her breasts pushing her tan shirt beautifully tight, imprinting two faint circles onto the fabric.

"Met somebody who knows your family," Fargo said. "Willie Baxter."

Alberta gave a snort. "That old fool?" she said.

"Is that what he is?" Fargo asked, surprised by her remark.

"Yes. He's an old coot who can't separate truth from his own inventions and delusions," Alberta said.

Fargo smiled. "He didn't have much good to say about your pa, either."

"Of course not. He's always accused Father of cheating him out of that mine he had. But then, he makes up all sorts of stories about everyone. That's his way of making himself feel important. He gets people to listen to him that way," Alberta said, more pity than anger in her tone.

"He's not wrong about everything," Fargo said, and Alberta questioned with an upraised eyebrow. "The traffic in Chinese slave labor."

"It's exaggerated," Alberta said.

"The Chinese I found hung by the roadside was no exaggeration. Neither was the shipload of slave labor I happened onto," Fargo said.

"I didn't say it doesn't occur. I said it's exaggerated.

People make more of it than it is. People like Willie Baxter," Alberta said.

"Maybe you just don't want to see it," Fargo offered.

"Why would I fool myself?" she returned.

"Some things are too upsetting to face," Fargo said, not ungently.

She thought for a moment, then let a wry smile edge her lips. "You're very perceptive," she murmured. "I suppose that's part of being the Trailsman, seeing things others don't see." She leaned forward and he found her lips pressing his, lingering, full and soft, then pulling away. "For being understanding, and for the first trail," she said softly.

"Bonus?" he said.

"Down payment," she answered and this time the hazel eyes definitely held a quiet fire. She rose, cutting off the moment. "You're welcome to spend the night here. I've plenty of extra room," she said.

"I'll take a rain check on that. I want to get an early start in the morning," he said and she walked outside into the dusk with him, waiting as he climbed into the saddle. A faint breeze blew the hazel hair. Lovely and touched with promise, he noted silently, a surprise more than worth hurrying back for.

"Good luck, and don't listen to old men with their delusions," she called as he rode away.

4

He found a small arbor just as night descended, set out his bedroll, finished a strip of cold beef jerky, and lay down. Alberta intruded on his thoughts to hold sleep away. Her disdainful dismissal of Willie Baxter stayed with him. Willie didn't seem the kind to traffic in delusions and exaggerations or wild stories. There didn't appear to be any rant or raving in him and he'd acted decisively when he had to, his take on the Chinese village sympathetically understanding. Alberta's derision didn't fit. Perhaps it was simply defensiveness of her father, Fargo reflected. Yet he couldn't dismiss one thing she'd said and he put it into a corner of his mind to think about at another time. Closing his eyes, he slept and the night was still and he was in the saddle with the new day.

He found a trail that was well worn and grunted to himself, certain the task wouldn't unfold that easily. The trail led northeast and by midmorning he came upon a long, shallow hillside and he slowed, taking in the flocks of sheep that covered the slope as though they were a carpet of cotton. A house and corrals occupied the top of the hillside, a horse and mule that Fargo recognized at once outside the house. Steering the pinto up the long hill, skirting the sheep, he saw three boys, ten to fourteen years of age he guessed, spread out watching the flocks, each with a rifle in hand. He reached the house and Willie Baxter came from the rear as Fargo reined to a halt, a smile rearranging his crinkles. "By God, didn't figure to see you so soon again," Willie said. "The Ryersons called me to help fix the pump on their back well."

"I was passing, saw your mule," Fargo said. "Wanted to ask you about something."

"Go ahead."

"When you were telling me about old man Foster, you never mentioned him cheating you out of a mine," Fargo said.

Willie gave a hard laugh. "You been talking to Alberta," he said.

"Yes," Fargo admitted.

"And you're wondering if that's why I ran her pa down," Willie said.

"It crossed my mind," Fargo said. "Carrying a grudge can color a man's feelings."

"That's why I didn't mention it. I knew you might think that," Willie said.

"You don't hold a grudge?" Fargo asked.

"I sure as hell do," Willie shot back candidly. "It just doesn't change anything I said about him. Being cheated by him just makes me one of many. It doesn't make me wrong about him."

"Not necessarily," Fargo agreed. "Just thought I'd clear the air."

"Any time," Willie said brightly.

"Thanks for listening," Fargo said. "See you again."

Turning the horse, he rode down the slope, again skirting the flocks of sheep and returned to the trail and rode north. The trail quickly vanished, the landscape swallowing it up with the same dense greenery he had found on his way to the coast. Once more he found himself using all the experience and trail wisdom he had stored inside him. Eventually he came upon passages that would serve as a stage trail with some chopping and pruning. The night came and he had but the beginnings of a map set down and he went to sleep feeling irritated. This land of Oregon resisted man's intrusions. It was little wonder so many wagon trains found not a future but despair when they finally reached this far west.

Morning came and he continued to explore. It took him another three days before he was able to map out a feasible trail. Without landmarks, and the land entirely new to him, it was hard to gauge how far he'd explored, but when he drew to a halt at the end of the third day he guessed he had come some fifty miles, give or take some. He surveyed the land and grimaced. Distant rolling hills, heavily timbered, rose up in all directions and he felt he had come upon a place that was really no place. To the north, he saw a high lake that sparkled in the late day's sun. It was a pristine spot, wildly beautiful, in the middle of nowhere. Even if a town were built he couldn't see how it could attract enough travelers for a stage line. He failed to see much future for Alberta's plans but he decided he'd not shoot holes in her dreams when he returned. Time and reality would do that.

He'd give her the trails she wanted for the dreams she had embraced. Once again, he started to retrace steps after marking the spot with a length of broken log he pounded into the ground. As he rode, he surveyed the terrain again. There were places that could be developed with hard work, flat areas where a ranch could be established. But these would hardly require a stagecoach line to service and he put away his own thoughts to concentrate on rechecking his map, adding and clarifying marks until he was satisfied with the finished chart. The trek back had consumed the better part of three days when he finally reached the long, sloping hillside where the floods of sheep still covered the land. He saw the three young boys starting to shepherd the sheep into their long corrals near the house and he saw something else in surprise: Willie Baxter's mule and horse still beside the house.

Fargo started to send the Ovaro up the hillside when Willie Baxter came from the house and hurried toward him. "Didn't expect you'd still be here," Fargo said as he halted.

"Been here waiting for you," Willie said, pushing the battered black derby back further on his head. "I knew I'd never find you if I went out looking for you so I stayed here. She's been taken."

Fargo felt the frown instantly dig into his brow as he asked the single word even as he feared he'd no need to. "Who?"

"The Chinese girl . . . Mei Ling. I visited the village to check on the work I'd done and they told me," Willie said.

"Goddamn," Fargo bit out. "How long ago?"

"Two days," Willie said.

"Anybody know anything, where, when, who?" Fargo questioned.

"I figure it had to be Bart Egan," Willie said.

"That an educated guess?" Fargo asked.

"More. A man, very big and very bald, was seen with her. That had to be Kurt Conroy, Egan's muscle man. They call him Big Baldy," Willie said.

"That's enough. I can spell out the rest," Fargo said and wheeled the Ovaro in a tight circle, sending the horse into a downhill gallop.

"Watch yourself. They're all bad actors," Willie called after him. Fargo lifted a hand as he raced on. He reached the bottom of the hill and turned the horse north toward Badger Hollow. It was night when he reached the town. There were still a few wide-wheeled logging trucks on the street but the town was dark and still, except for the saloon and Fargo reined up outside the two-store structure, tethered the Ovaro to the hitching post, and stepped through the swinging door. Inside, he saw a very average saloon, fairly well crowded, a dozen tables, and a long bar. A half-dozen girls in short, shiny dresses with low-cut necks sat near the back wall, and an older woman with some attractiveness still lingering in her face surveyed the room from a rear table.

Fargo saw her rise as he strolled toward her. He paused to glance at the bar, where a short man in shirt-sleeves also took him in from behind the bar. "Hello, stranger," the woman said. "I'm Monica. What's your pleasure?"

"That depends," Fargo said quietly, surveying the room again. He saw no bald head and he lowered himself onto a chair at the table. "Looking for Bart Egan," he said.

The woman smiled, letting him take in the heavy

breasts that overflowed the neck of the tight, black dress she wore. "He's out of town for a few days," she said. "You don't need Bart. I can see to anything you want."

"How about Big Baldy?" Fargo asked.

"He's not here, either," the madam said.

"Anybody expected back?" Fargo asked.

"Can't say when." The woman shrugged. "Why don't you take a room and wait? We've some young ladies who'll make it very enjoyable."

Fargo thought for a moment. "I'd want something special, really special," he said.

"All of our girls are special," the madam said.

Fargo's smile was cold. "No games, honey. You know what I mean. Special, different, such as a nice, young China girl."

She kept her face carefully composed. "Guess you'd have to see Bart about that when he gets back," she said.

"Too bad. I'm ready to pay good money right now," he said and watched her closely.

"Sorry," she said, her face still a careful mask. She was turning him away and he wondered why. Didn't she know about Mei Ling? That didn't seem possible. Had she been told not to offer her? That explanation didn't sit well with him, Fargo pondered. "I'm sure we've a girl who'd satisfy you," the woman said.

"I'll think on it. Meanwhile, I'll have a bourbon and something to eat," Fargo said.

"Buffalo sandwich?"

"That'll be fine," Fargo said and sat back in the chair. He'd have to use up time now, he decided as he nursed the bourbon along with the sandwich. He had just finished his second bourbon as the last of the bar patrons left. Rising, Fargo paid the check, and found the madam at his side as he started to leave.

"Sure you won't stay?" she asked.

"Maybe tomorrow," he said and strolled from the saloon. Outside, he rode the Ovaro into the night. Slipping into a narrow alleyway between buildings, he left the horse in the narrow blackness. Stepping into the street, Fargo stayed against the building line, halted opposite the saloon, and watched as the lights went out one by one in the second floor of the structure. When the building was dark, he crossed the street at a crouch and made his way to the right corner where he had already picked out the drainpipe that ran up the building to the roof. Metal bands every few feet around the pipe jutted out enough to provide hand and toeholds and Fargo pulled himself up the pipe. Reaching the second floor, he could lean over to the nearest window, which was slightly open at the bottom. He clung to the windowsill, got one leg up enough to give him leverage, and slowly, carefully, raised the window until he could slide into the room. He rested on his hands and knees, letting his eyes become accustomed to the darkness while he listened to the steady breathing of deep sleep from the figure in the single bed.

Rising to his feet, he crossed the room on silent steps, his eyes glancing at the girl in the bed. She didn't wake and he silently opened the door and slipped out into the hall. A dim lamp let him see the row of doors on each side of a hallway and he swore silently as he stepped to the nearest door. He closed one big hand around the doorknob, silently eased the door open, and peered into the dark room. He heard the deep breathing of sleep and closed the door and went on to the one across the hall. He did the same, carefully edging it open just enough to peer inside and listen, proceeding on to the next door and then the next until he had only one door left at the end of the hall.

Again, he opened the door just enough to peer in. Unlike all the other rooms, which had been small, single rooms, this one was twice the size with a double-sized bed and big dresser and a loveseat. He stepped into the room, closed the door after him, and crossed to the large bed near the window where the moonlight let him see the madam's face as she slept on her back. He reached down, put his hand over the woman's mouth, and she woke at once, her eyes snapping open in surprise and fright. She took a moment to focus on him and he saw recognition come into her eyes. "Don't scream or it'll be your last one, understand?" Fargo said and she nodded. He drew his hand back and she sat up, the sheet falling from her. She wore nothing underneath and her large breasts swayed as she drew in deep breaths.

"What're you doing here? This your way of not paying for your fun?" the woman said.

Fargo almost laughed. She could see the world only one way. "Once a madam always a madam," he said. "No, I'm here for the answers you didn't give me before. Big Baldy has the Chinese girl. Where are they?"

"I don't know," she said.

Fargo closed one hand around her throat. "Don't make me do something I don't want to do," he growled and saw fear quickly flood her face. She was used to men who'd think nothing at killing. She'd no reason to suppose he wasn't one.

"He took her to Rough Rock," the woman said.

Fargo drew his hand from around her throat. "What's that?"

"A town northwest of here. Bart has another saloon there," the woman said.

"Why'd he take her there?" Fargo questioned.

"It's where he takes all the girls who don't want to co-operate. After a week at Rough Rock they come around fast," the madam said.

"Bastard. That includes you," Fargo spit out.

"I don't like it. I can't stop it, though," the woman said.

"Where is it?" Fargo asked.

"Take the road northwest from here. Stay on it. You'll come to it."

"How far?"

"Riding hard, you could reach it by midmorning," the madam said.

He put a hand on her collarbone and pushed her back onto the bed and her big breasts bounced. "Go back to sleep," he said and saw her frown up at him, surprise and questions in her eyes. "What's the matter?" he asked. "Not sleepy anymore?"

"How do you know I won't send some of Bart's boys after you?" she asked.

"You can't, not without admitting what you told me. That wouldn't make your boss happy, would it?" he said and tossed her a smile. She glowered back, pulled the sheet around herself, and turned her back to him. He crossed the room in three long strides, hurrying into the hallway and outside. Retrieving the Ovaro in the alleyway, he took the road north out of town. He rode hard and stopped only when his fatigue refused to be ignored. He found a spot off the road and bedded down, aware that sleep was a necessity not a luxury. He'd no idea what he'd run into in Rough Rock and he'd need to be alert and at his best.

Sleeping at once, he woke only when the warmth of the morning sun touched his face. He found a stand of wild plums for breakfast and soon moved north again. Holding to a steady pace, he unhappily watched the sun cross the noon sky. It was midafternoon when he rode into the town, where he saw the huge rock of granite that rose up to give the town its name. The town itself was even more primitive than Badger Hollow, the buildings crude and ramshackle, the single main street crowded with boisterous lumberjacks already half drunk. The saloon, the largest structure in town, had customers spilling in and out of it. Fargo drew to a halt, his eyes going to a smaller building attached to one side of the saloon where a man stood in front of the closed doorway, plainly guarding the entrance. Fargo casually moved on. He started into the saloon and stepped aside for two lumberjacks, easy to recognize by their heavy leather belts.

He was about to enter the saloon when he saw the man coming along behind him, huge, three hundred pounds, Fargo guessed, a massive head shaved completely bald, the face beneath it made of blue eyes that seemed smaller than they were in the massive folds of fat, thick lips, and swaying jowls. The man's head fitted onto his shoulders with no apparent neck in between. Fargo saw him slow to look long and sharply at the Ovaro. Fargo gave little thought to that. People often paused to admire the perfection of the Ovaro with its classic jet black fore-and-hindquarters and pure white midsection. Fargo proceeded into the saloon, conscious of the man following.

He had found Big Baldy. Mei Ling had to be near, he felt certain. The saloon interior was a dismal place, with paint-chipped walls and weathered ceiling timbers, as rundown as its customers and worn as the four girls that watched him enter. He sat down at a table at the far end of the room. Big Baldy had halted at the bar where two men immediately moved over to him. One of the girls moved to Fargo, her eyes tired and weary. "Bourbon," he ordered and let his eyes travel around the room, pausing on the curtained doorway at the rear of the room that faced the adjoining building. He waited, sipped the bourbon, seeming to be but one more customer as he let the saloon grow more crowded. But his eyes continued to flick to Big Baldy, who continued in animated conversation with his two companions.

Finally, Fargo rose, left the table, and sauntered around the room, halting to watch a five-handed poker game, then drifted on until he was at the curtain entranceway. Another quick glance at Big Baldy showed the man still at the bar and Fargo took a step backward, slipping through the curtain and finding himself in a short corridor. A closed door at the end of the corridor had to lead to the attached structure, he was certain, and moving quickly, he reached the door. Finding it unlocked, he pulled it open. He stepped into a square area, which was divided into four boxlike cubicles. Three doors hung open and he saw each cubicle held a mattress on the floor and a water basin. The fourth door was closed and he crossed over to it. He listened, and hearing nothing, he carefully pulled it open. Inside, it was the same as the other cubicles, but a figure lay on the cot, ankles and wrists bound. Fargo stepped inside. Mei Ling's head lifted, her eyes widening as she saw him. He put a finger to his lips and her mouth stayed open but she made no sound as he knelt down and untied the ropes. She flung her arms around him when he finished. As she clung to him, he noticed that her slender figure held no trembling.

"What did they do to you?" Fargo asked.

"They hit me, in the stomach and in the back. They were careful not to leave marks," Mei Ling whispered. "I told them I'd never do what they wanted of me. They said I would when they were through with me."

"Can you stand?" he asked and she nodded. She rose, clinging to him. He brought her to the door and halted, his lips tightening. It was more than likely the guard was still outside and he'd react the moment the door was opened. "Stay here. Come out when I open the door," he said. He left her and returned to the curtained doorway. He parted one edge and peered out, his eyes going to the bar. Big Baldy and the two men were gone and Fargo pushed through the curtain. He strode from the saloon and paused outside the door as he scanned the street. There was no sign of the huge bald-headed figure and he decided to leave the Ovaro at the hitching post. Sliding along the wall of the building, he turned the corner to the smaller adjoining building. He had guessed right, the guard was still outside the door.

Strolling casually, Fargo moved toward the man and was almost abreast of him, his hand resting on the butt of the Colt at his hip when the voice came from behind him. "That's far enough," it said. Fargo halted, his every muscle tensing. Slowly, he turned to see Big Baldy and the two men, all with guns drawn and leveled at him. He grimaced. Taking another second to weigh the odds, his eyes flicked to the guard, who had also drawn his gun. Four of them, at close range, all with guns already aimed. Fargo let a deep breath whistle through his lips and relaxed his body. The odds were impossible to overcome and he remained still as one of the men came up and took the Colt from him.

Big Baldy's face creased in a sneering smile. "Figured all I had to do was wait and watch," he said.

Fargo's eyes bored into the man. "Lucky guess?" he questioned.

"No. I know who you are. You're Fargo," the man said and Fargo felt his brows raise. "You're the one who left the message with Sam Bundy," the big man went on. "Sam and I talk. He told me about it and how his man said you rode a real fine Ovaro. I knew it was you soon as I saw the horse."

"Guess it doesn't always pay to have a fine horse," Fargo said blandly.

"It doesn't pay to poke your nose into other people's business," Big Baldy threw back. Fargo made no reply as his thoughts raced inside him. The double-edged throwing knife was in its calf holster but it might just as well not be there. He'd no way to use it now. He'd need time and an opportunity for that. "Get her," Big Baldy snapped at the guard and Fargo winced inwardly as the guard pulled the door open and Mei Ling rushed out.

She halted, dismay flooding her face. He refused to feed into the crushed shock he saw there.

"Change of plans," he said calmly.

"Son of a bitch, you got a smart mouth, Fargo," Big Baldy said, and barking at his men, two of them seized Fargo, pushing him along as they followed Big Baldy around to the front of the saloon. Fargo saw the guard bringing Mei Ling as Baldy halted in the wide street in front of the saloon and a crowd of curious onlookers gathered at once. A fifth man appeared, handed Big Baldy an object, and Fargo saw it was a bullwhip. Big Baldy uncurled it to its ten-foot length.

He knew full well how a bullwhip could tear flesh to ribbons, bringing an excruciatingly painful death. But instead of defeat and despair, he felt the moment of hope spiral through him, aware of the incongruousness of it. But he had just been given a kind of reprieve, time handed to him. Time that would be wrapped in pain, he knew, but he'd still welcome it. Big Baldy liked to inflict pain on his victims. A bullet was too unsatisfying for him. He needed that special thrill of torture, torment, and pain, the pleasures of the sadist, and Fargo found himself feeling ironically grateful for the perverse pleasures of sadism.

At a signal from Big Baldy, two of his men stripped the jacket and shirt from Fargo. The man wanted to enjoy the sight as well as the sound of flesh and blood being torn and Fargo's eyes peered at the huge form. Big Baldy's fat lips were quivering in anticipation. The crowd of onlookers had tripled, he saw, and he also knew he could expect no help from any of them. Many undoubtedly had their own hidden streaks of sadism which they could now vicariously enjoy. Besides, Big Baldy was a presence in town few would want to challenge. The moving folds of flesh stepped forward, snapped the bullwhip into the air with a loud crack, then sent the plaited whip curling at his victim. Fargo, using the agility and timing he possessed, managed to avoid the whip, skidded sideways, and had his feet in position as Big Baldy struck again. Once more, Fargo avoided the whip's lash but felt the air crackle alongside him.

Big Baldy grunted as he let the whip fly again, and this time Fargo felt the very tip of it nick his leg as he half turned and spun. He couldn't avoid the crackling lash very much longer, he realized. Big Baldy was snapping the bullwhip out faster. Yet Fargo, dropping to his hands and knees, avoided the whip again, and whirled away and straightened. Big Baldy sent the bullwhip sideways, a sudden, unexpected maneuver, and Fargo tried twisting away. Realizing he couldn't avoid the whip, he tensed his body as the lash curled around his back. The pain, sharp and intense, made him grit his teeth and he reached for the whip but Big Baldy had drawn it back. Facing the man, Fargo feinted from left to right with his body. His attempt to draw Baldy into a mistake failed. The bullwhip cracked out, slashed into his ribs, and Fargo felt the pain as a gash opened in his skin.

Again, he tried to get one hand on the end of the whip but Big Baldy knew how to use the weapon. He snaked it away, yanked it back, and lashed out again. Fargo cursed as the whip tore another slash in his side. He spun and missed a grab at the whip as Big Baldy snaked it aside. Spinning again, he tried to dive to his left but the whip cracked out again, the pain this time a searing, burning moment of agony that made him stumble. He tried to recover, managed to spin away but the bullwhip lashed out again, curling around him as it ripped open a long gash all the way across his chest. He felt the blood spray over him as he dropped to one knee, and rose again only to feel the whip slice deep into his back. He got a hand on the end of the lash but felt it slip through his fingers as Baldy pulled. The man was lashing out furiously now, again and again, and Fargo steeled himself against the pain as he let out curses, managing to avoid the full force of some of the lashes. But the pain came in waves and he felt the moments of weakness pull at him.

He tried turning his shoulders, buttocks, twisting his legs, anything to avoid the full impact of the whip again. Twice, he managed to get hold of the lash, only to have it yanked away. But he saw Big Baldy was puffing, drawing deep breaths, his face wreathed in perspiration that dripped down his swaying jowls. The fat he carried was taking its toll on his exertions and he was growing careless, missing more with his lashes. He stepped closer, struck out, and missed again, and this time Fargo's foot came down on the end of the whip. He dived forward, wrapped both hands around the whip and pulled, finding a reservoir of strength from deep inside him.

Big Baldy, his hand wrapped around the other end of the whip, fell forward onto both knees. With a roar of surprise and rage, he tried to regain his feet, still holding on to his end of the whip. Fargo swung from one knee, a long, looping left, followed with an equally long right delivered with all the strength left in him. Both blows landed flush on the man's jaw. Big Baldy's fat face shook, his jowls jiggling as he quivered and fell backward, the whip falling from his hand. It was the moment he needed, Fargo realized, probably the only one he'd have. He dove forward as he yanked the blade from its calf holster, landed on the mountainous form, the edge of the blade digging into the man's throat. Big Baldy's eyes widened in fear as he felt the sharp edge of the knife. Staying half atop the man, Fargo rasped orders over his shoulder. "Drop your guns," he ordered. "Now, or I cut his fat, bald head off."

"Jesus, do it, do what he says," Baldy said as Fargo pressed the blade harder into the man's throat. Fargo's eyes went to the men, who reluctantly let their guns drop to the ground.

"Mei Ling, get my gun," Fargo ordered. The slender form darted past him and picked up the Colt. "Get the horse," Fargo said, keeping the blade hard against Big Baldy's throat. Mei Ling ran by and returned, leading the Ovaro. Fargo drew a deep breath, and fought off an attack of dizziness as he felt the blood running down his torso from a dozen tears and gouges. Drawing the knife from the man's throat, Fargo pushed to his feet, took the Colt from Mei Ling, and reached one hand up to the saddle horn. He paused, gathering the strength to pull himself onto the Ovaro. The sound registered in his ears, the rustle of a shirt. He half turned to see Big Baldy drawing the pistol out from inside his shirt.

Fargo fired the Colt from where he leaned against the Ovaro. The man's bald head erupted in a shower of scarlet as he turned into a grotesque, bulbous figure with something that resembled a giant beet atop it. Fighting off another wave of dizziness, Fargo pulled himself onto the horse. He groaned in pain as Mei Ling helped him. She climbed onto the horse behind him as he swept Baldy's men with the Colt. They didn't move, their eyes fixed on the grotesque, lifeless figure. Fargo sent the Ovaro into a trot, rode through the onlookers that parted for him, fought away more waves of pain-filled dizziness, and rode from the town in the last light of the day.

He slowed when he was far enough from town. Mei Ling was supporting him, her arms around him, her body pressed to him. On the way to the town he had noted a small lake between two low hills, and now found the strength to make his way to it, where he found thick mountain ash growing almost to the very shores. He slid from the saddle, Mei Ling helping him. Sinking to the shore, he pulled his way into the lake and lay in the cool water, letting it wash the blood from him. Dimly, he saw Mei Ling rummaging in his saddlebag. Finally she returned with towels and an old shirt she tore into strips. Pulling himself almost out of the water in the gathering dusk, he lay on his stomach and felt the pain shooting through his body from the tears in his flesh.

"There's a horn bottle," he began.

"Yes, I saw it," she interrupted.

"Get it," he murmured. "Rub the salve over the cuts." He lay half in the water as she returned with the bottle, pulling himself entirely onto the land and letting her draw the rest of his clothes from him. He closed his eyes as she began to rub the salve gently over each slash in his body.

"What am I rubbing on?" she asked.

"Balm of Gilead, comfrey, hyssop, birch bark compress," he said.

"We use many herbs and plants in my homeland," Mei Ling said. "There are some in the village that were brought over. They will help you." He nodded, wincing at a particularly sore slash, but still managing to admire the gentleness of her touch. The salve felt soothing immediately and after applying it she wrapped a piece of cloth over each cut. When she turned him onto his back to tend to the tears in his chest, abdomen, and legs, he saw her black eyes pause as they took in the muscled beauty of his body, lingering for a moment longer at particular places. She bent to the task again, gently rubbing in the salve, putting a cloth over each wound when she finished. "You're very good," Fargo said. "I'm grateful you're here."

"I'm the grateful one," she said. "Can you sleep some?" He nodded and she helped him under the small, white-flowered leaves of an old ash. "My dress is covered with blood. I'll wash it out in the lake. You sleep."

"That won't take much doing," Fargo said, and closing his eyes as darkness fell, he listened to Mei Ling at the edge of the little lake, and then plunged into a deep sleep. He didn't open his eyes until the morning sun came, turning his head to see Mei Ling beside him, wrapped in a blanket from his saddlebag. She woke, keeping the blanket around her as she took the now-clean and dry dress from a low branch. She slipped behind a tree and returned with the garment clinging to her lovely slenderness. She helped him pull on trousers, boots, and shirt.

"Can we make it to Han Village?" Mei Ling asked.

"Real slowly," Fargo said and she climbed into the saddle behind him. He didn't realize how slow the trip would be until he found he had to stop entirely too often to rest, his body still wracked with searing pain. In between stops he skirted Badger Hollow, staying off the few traveled roads. The second night had fallen when he and Mei Ling reached Han Village. The comfort the salve brought was the only thing that let him withstand the physical strain of riding where even the Ovaro's slowest steps jarred and pulled on his torn muscles. Mei Ling called others who helped him out of the saddle at the village and he was taken into a small hut and lay down on a cot.

"Rest," he heard Mei Ling say and felt her taking off his clothes and strips of bandage. He closed his eyes and slept at once, staying sound asleep until the night was deep. He woke, saw the candle in a corner of the small hut that gave a soft light to the room, and then found Mei Ling's figure as she sat up on his bedroll and came to him. Her hand on his forehead was soothing, smooth. "You had a fever. It is gone," she said. "Sleep does wonderful things."

He pushed up on one elbow, wincing with the effort. A sheet atop him fell away and he saw he was naked. Mei Ling turned to a small table with a number of objects on it, a clay pot and a cup and an iron stand with a base of glowing embers that kept the clay pot hot. "I've some things for you," she said and he sat up straighter as she poured from the pot, a green-tinted liquid, handed him the cup. *"Fo-ti-tieng,"* she said. "A wonderful herb brought from China. Drink." He sipped from the cup, found a not-unpleasant taste, a little smoky with a quiet strength to it. "An ancient Chinese herbalist, Li Chung Yun, lived for two hundred and fifty-six years drinking *fo-ti-tieng* and ginseng every day."

"I've heard of ginseng," Fargo said between sips. "I think it's grown in this country in places."

"I have a cup of ginseng for you to take when you finish the *fo-ti-tieng*," Mei Ling said. "But this is the wild variety, *schinseng*. It is best, the most effective." He handed her the empty cup and she filled it with the gingseng tea, and watched him drink it slowly. When he finished, she stacked everything neatly on the small table. "There is a latrine beside the hut. I will come back in the morning with more of everything for you." She paused, her hand touching his cheek. "I put more salve on your cuts when you were asleep," she said. He caught her hand and pressed the palm to his lips before he let it go. A small light danced in her black eyes as she left, carrying the table with effortless, silent grace. He closed his eyes and slept at once, waking only to go outside and return until the new day arrived.

A washbasin had been placed inside the hut, he saw as he swung long legs from the cot, two cloths beside it. When he finished he lay down again and Mei Ling appeared with the small table of tea, this time accompanied by sliced oranges. "I feel better," he said when he finished.

"Drink and tomorrow you will feel even better," she said and sat at the edge of the cot. She wore another one-piece dress that fitted her willowy shape and somehow managed to be both demure and provocative. The tea had an enervating effect and he slept again, only dimly aware of her leaving. He woke and it was night, the candle glowing softly. He rose, surprised at how the whip-marks had almost stopped hurting. There were two teas waiting on the table for him. He drank both as he wondered where Mei Ling was and realized he was disappointed by her absence. Returning to the cot, he slept again and woke with the late-afternoon sun slanting into the open door of the hut. Finding his shirt and jeans washed and dried and laid out and waiting for him, he drew on the jeans and went to the door to peer out.

Once again, he found himself waiting for Mei Ling to visit but all he saw were the figures tending the vegetable patches. Stepping back into the hut, he was surprised at how well he felt and he lay on the cot, dozed, and woke again to find night had descended, the candle glowing inside the hut. Automatically, he looked to see if Mei Ling was there but he was alone. He wondered about her. She'd not stayed away this long since bringing him here. He was still thinking about her when a young Chinese boy entered with a platter with a wooden basket on it, small curls of steam rising from inside the basket. The boy placed the platter on the table, half bowed, and backed out of the hut. Lifting the cover, Fargo peered into the basket, which held rice with a dark sauce on it and steamed dumplings. He ate slowly, savoring the meal, and had finished when the boy returned and took away the platter.

Mei Ling still hadn't come to visit and Fargo lay down on the cot, Mei Ling staying in his thoughts. But after a few moments he felt the smile come to his lips. She had ministrated to him, brought him wondrous teas to help him recover, and had stayed away. But she had faith the things brought him would have their effect, combined with rest. Perhaps more than faith, he mused. Perhaps the wisdom of the Orient, herbal and philosophical. His smile stayed. Her absence had been part of that wisdom, he was convinced now. Silence was not always simply silence. Sometimes it was its own kind of message.

He was suddenly not concerned with why, only when. The smile was still edging his lips when he opened his eyes at the sound and saw the slender figure coming into the hut, pulling the drape closed over the entranceway. She halted at the cot, clothed in the simple dress that was still both demure and clinging. He took in the lovely delicacy of her features, the finely etched lips, the black eyes that seemed to simmer, the smooth cheekbones that gave strength to delicacy. She noted the little smile on his lips. "Good," she said, answering with her own smile. "You have come to understand," she said.

"I think so," he said, sitting up.

"Then you know I have not come out of gratefulness," she said.

"I know," he nodded. "And I'm glad."

Her smile stayed, disappearing only for a moment as she lifted both arms, pulling the dress over her head and letting it fall to the floor. He felt his breath draw in at the naked beauty of her.

5

She stood very quietly, very straight, yet there was no boastfulness, no display in her, just a quiet statement, beauty for its own sake, beauty its own reason for being. His eyes feasted on a figure that somehow combined willow-wand slenderness with soft curvaceousness. A long, graceful neck curved down to smooth, round shoulders. Breasts that seemed not smallish at all but perfect on her long figure, high and firm, full enough at the bottoms to give each a saucy upturn, each lovely mound topped by a dark pink tip centered on a very small areola of matching tint.

A prominent rib cage descended into a long, narrow waist that slid downward to a flat abdomen, a small, elliptical indentation in the very center, somehow provocative in itself. Beneath it, the soft swell of her surprised him, an unexpected little sensuous mound that dipped down to a triangle so small it hardly existed. It almost made her seem a little girl but the very womanly curve of her Venus mound denied that at once. Her legs, beautifully slender yet not thin, completed the willowed perfection of her. She slid down beside him, her arms lifting to encircle his neck and his hands felt the smoothness of her, skin that was warm and instantly exciting to the touch. He looked into jet eyes that were suddenly black fire, a startling contrast to the quiet beauty of the rest of her. They flashed black commands at him as she brought her finely etched lips onto his, pressing, lingering soft yet firm and the tip of her tongue darted forward, tantalizing, tempting. He opened his mouth for her, matching her eagerness.

Drawing back, he slid his lips down the long neck, moving slowly over one soft-firm breast, found the dark pink little tip, and tasted of it. "Ah . . . aaaaah," Mei Ling breathed and he circled the nipple with his tongue, causing it to expand in his mouth as he drew more of the silk-smooth breast in. Mei Ling's soft sighs grew stronger as he sucked on the sweet mound, went to the other, and then back again. His hand slowly crept downward, across the smooth abdomen, pausing at the oblong little indentation, and going on to come to the small rise of the curvaceous little belly. "Yes . . . yes," Mei Ling gasped and he moved down further, to the smooth, almost hairless pubic mound. As he caressed the smooth softness of it, her sighs rose with a new urgency. He caressed and savored the feel of her, the little hairs covering his fingers, giving their own erotic flavor and Mei Ling sighed again, and again, and again. She half turned toward him, her legs lifting, parting, beckoning.

He reached down, touched the warm moistness, and her thighs snapped together as she gave a sharp sigh, holding him inside the soft, warm hollow, sighing with pleasure. Then her thighs suddenly parted again, as the petals of a flower fall open. He moved forward, deeper into the deliquescent path and her sighs were imbued with new flavor, a new fervor. He felt her hands along his body, caresses as soft as if a butterfly's wing were fluttering up and down his body, terribly delicate and terribly sensuous. He half turned and brought his muscled body, his throbbing maleness to rest against her, heard her long, shuddering sigh, something between disbelief and delight. Her thighs opened, clasped around him, beautifully moist, and her gasps were coming in quick succession. Again, her hands fluttered and flicked across his back, her slender loveliness surging with him, long legs encircling his hips, smooth Venus mound tight against him. Her high, firm breasts pressed into him, and found his face as she lifted herself upward, staying against him.

No cries, no screams of ecstasy, no wild moans or groans, none of that came from her, only the long, curling sighs. But what wonderful sighs that rose and fell, stretched and shortened, each echoing ecstasy in a hundred susurrant ways, each a quiet cry of absolute pleasure. She lay locked with him, as if together they might infuse each other, become a single entity of rapture. But as her sighs were a quiet measure of passion, he felt her slender body become a pulsing, quivering organ, her legs straightening, lifting again, rubbing against him. Suddenly he felt her tightening, the character of her sighs changing, a new abruptness taking hold of them, sighs becoming gasps, one after the other. Her fingers were digging into his back, every part of her growing more intense, and he felt himself joining her, expanding, exploding, all the erotic, passionate sensations coming together. Then, in one startling outburst, the sighs shattered, replaced by a quick, high-pitched shriek that ended as quickly as it erupted.

But she clung to him, silk-smooth skin against him and he felt her contractions go on, finally slowing but continuing until finally they ended, subsiding as her body reluctantly released itself from the grip of pleasure. Her long legs stayed clasped to him, her breasts pushing against his face, sweet little tips against his lips. "*Yíqiè . . . yíqiè . . .* everything . . . everything, more than I could hope," she murmured, pulled back, her hands clasping his face. "But not more than I expected," she added, laughter dancing in the black eyes. She curled against him. "Sleep with me. I want you against me until the night is gone." He lay down beside her and she brought one leg over his groin, one piquant breast to his mouth and he heard her sigh of contentment. He closed his eyes and felt pretty damn contented himself.

Wrapped in her warm, smooth loveliness, he slept till the new sun woke him and stirred him into wakefulness. Mei Ling opened her eyes. She stretched with languorous beauty as he watched and knew he'd not get up until she did. But she pushed onto her elbows, breasts saucily thrusting upward, then sat up. Her smile was rueful as she read his thoughts. "I don't want to go, either," she said. "But I must. Mr. Ryan sends a man to go with me, now. I must be ready when he arrives." She stretched again and he felt his breath draw in at the sheer loveliness of her. "A letter came to Mr. Han, sent months ago from China. It said three boats of new immigrants are on their way here," she said, her face growing sober. "I hope they will not experience what I did but I am afraid for them."

"Why?" Fargo questioned.

"The letter said they were sailing on ships of Portuguese traders," she told him.

"Let's hope these three aren't the same as the one you sailed on," he said with more reassurance than he felt. He sat up as she stood to draw her dress on.

"Your friend, the old man, came to visit when you were recovering," Mei Ling said.

"Willie Baxter," Fargo said and she nodded.

"He said to tell you to come see him when you were better," she went on.

"How'd he know I was here?" Fargo asked.

"He said he passed through Rough Rock. People were still talking about what happened," she said. Fargo grunted, not surprised. She came to him and held him against her. "You'll be gone before I return tonight, won't you?" she asked and he nodded. "Come back to me," she murmured.

"Soon as I can. Promise," he said.

"I stay in the third hut up the hill from here," she said. "I will be waiting every moment."

"I'll be back," he said. She turned, leaving as quickly and silently as the wind blows away a willow wand. He rose, found the Ovaro tethered outside, the saddle nearby, and he rode from the village, waving to those who waved as he passed. He decided to put off visiting Willie Baxter. He'd lost more days than he knew and he rode north before turning southeast. He'd stop at Alberta's place, where he was headed before everything had happened. He had the map of the second trail to give her before he started the third and last. But as he crossed the start of the trail to the coast, he saw the line of hoofprints moving along the new trail he'd broken. The riders were in no hurry, he noted, and saw three sets of prints deeper into the ground than the others.

Curious, he followed, frowning to himself as he followed into the afternoon, still seeing only the prints. He had marked the places where he felt the trail needed work, trees cut back, the land smoothed, rocks dug up and set aside. But nothing had been touched. If these prints were Alberta's men he wondered why they'd passed over the places he'd noted. Growing more curious, he kept on into the late afternoon, seeing other spots he had marked that had been left untouched, and realized he was almost halfway to the coast. Suddenly he heard the sound of hammers and saws and men's voices. When he rounded a curve, he came to a straight stretch where a knot of figures were erecting a house. They had the frame up and most of a low roof with two of the walls in place and he stared at a structure long and low, not unlike a barracks.

He rode to a halt and one of the men, tall with long hair tied into a ponytail, came toward him, a hammer in one hand. "I'm Anderson. Miss Foster send you?" he asked, one hand hooked into his coveralls.

"She tell you to come out here and build?" Fargo queried.

"She told us to pick a good spot. This seemed it," the man said.

"What are you building?" Fargo questioned.

"A way station," Anderson said.

Fargo's brows lifted. "A way station?" he echoed. "I'd think fixing the trail would come first."

"Miss Foster felt the way station would take longer

and should be put up first," the man said. "We don't argue with Miss Foster."

Fargo cast another long glance at the structure. "You boys ever build a way station before?" he asked.

Anderson's eyes grew wary. "It's not done. It'll be just right when it's finished," he said. Fargo nodded. It was an oblique answer, one that could conceal ulterior purpose or simple incompetence. Surveying the partly built structure again, he turned away.

"Good luck," he said as he rode away into the night that had descended. He slowed, picked his way carefully, and waited until the moon rose to afford enough light to find the trail. He thought about Alberta as he rode. She was plainly bent on putting her plans into effect as quickly as she could. She seemed also bent on going about things the wrong way. Building a way station before smoothing the trail was simply ridiculous planning. Building it before there were towns, places for travelers to visit, was even more wrongheaded. It was as though carving out trails and way stations would somehow push her dreams into becoming reality. It was a dangerous indulgence, one that could bring on disappointment and terrible bitterness. He'd bring it up to her, he decided. She needed a rein. She was being carried away on her own headlong ambitions.

He put away thoughts of Alberta Foster as he saw the moon nearing the midnight sky and decided to bed down. He chose a stand of red alder and slept soundly as the night remained quiet. He breakfasted on apples and wild cherries and continued along his trail as day came. It was late afternoon when he reached Alberta's place. One of the wagons was still there and a few less ranch hands. Alberta opened the door as he rode to a halt and dismounted and he saw her hazel eyes were cool, her face carefully composed as she regarded him with arms folded over a yellow shirt that pushed her breasts up.

She waited by the door as he approached, the map in his hand. "Your trail northeast," he said.

The coolness in her eyes didn't change, he saw as she took the map. "I expected you days ago," she said.

"Got sidetracked," he said.

"I know," she said, her glance coolly disapproving as his brows lifted. "You thought I wouldn't hear about Rough Rock?" she said.

"Didn't think about it," Fargo said.

"I'm paying you to find trails for me, not play Good Samaritan to little immigrant girls on my time," she said icily.

He felt surprise push into him. She could be coldly peremptory. "I'll remember that," he returned.

"Come in while I go over the map," Alberta said. He followed her into the house and sat down on the sofa beside her as she began to examine the map. A black skirt crept up to reveal nice knees, very round and attractive, no boniness to them whatever. She questioned him on certain markings, had him explain others, and so thoroughly went over the map, she had to turn on lamps as night fell. Finally finishing, she put the map into a drawer in a small table.

"I'll get at the last one come morning," Fargo said, getting to his feet.

"You're welcome to spend the night," she offered as she rose but the hazel eyes were still cool, her face still set. Strangely, it gave her a different kind of beauty, an iciness that somehow simmered, a contrast that created its own magnificence. "You'll be more comfortable here than in a bedroll," she added.

"No thanks," he said curtly, turned, and started from the room. He was at the door when she called out.

"You're angry with me," she said.

He paused at the door, tossed a glance back. "That's half right," he conceded.

"What's the other half?" she questioned.

"Disappointed," he said.

"Why?"

"I'm not much for ice queens," he tossed at her.

Her set features broke as she frowned and her lips parted. "I'm not an ice queen," she protested, rising.

"There's no caring in you," he said.

"Because of what I said?" she asked, coming to stand in front of him.

"Bull's-eye, honey," he said.

"I'd waited for you to come back, waited, thought about it, more than I realized," she said and her hands came to rest on his chest. He was taken aback as he saw the contrition in the hazel eyes. She rushed her words, let them tumble from her. "I'm possessive, jealous. I make quick attractions. It's a fault. I've no right. I know that but I do it. I was having my own fancies about your returning and then I hear you're off rescuing her. I let it get to me." Her arms came up, circled his neck. "I'm sorry. I run off with myself."

"You do, in more ways than this," he said. His hands held her waist as her arms stayed around his neck, feeling the soft fullness of her.

"How?" she asked and pulled him back to the sofa with her.

"You let your plans run off with you. You run off building way stations," Fargo told her but not harshly.

"You saw it?" She frowned in surprise.

"As much as was built. I passed by. Hell, Alberta, you don't have the trail ready. You don't even have a Concord and there isn't a new town for anyone to go to. But you're building a way station. That's really running off with yourself," Fargo said.

"A stage is supposed to be delivered next week," Alberta said.

He shrugged. "That doesn't much change things. You're still running far ahead of yourself," he told her.

She bit her lips ruefully. "All right, I do that. I've always done it. I get caught up in my own emotions. I want something, it consumes me."

"That can be dangerous," Fargo said.

"It can be dangerous," she said and her mouth came to his, pressed, and clung. "I've wanted you since the first time you rode in here. I was hurt when I heard about the Chinese girl. I reacted poorly. I'll make it up to you." She brought her mouth to his again, her lips very pliable, made for pleasure. "I'm being honest, telling you everything because I want you to help me, understand me, believe me," she said. Her mouth pressed his again, opening to take in his tongue. She was proving her words, letting desire reinforce contrition. He couldn't refuse or reject that, he told himself. It wouldn't be right.

He let his mouth meet her kisses, felt her answer at once. His hand touched the top of the yellow blouse, felt skin, and realized she had opened her buttons. He moved his touch downward, over the soft swell of her breasts. "Oh, yes, yes," Alberta murmured, and wriggling her shoulders, pushed the blouse off. The shoulder straps of her slip fell down and his eyes lingered on full, deep breasts, nipples a dark red centered on large, rosy circles, opulent, luscious breasts. His hand curled around one, and Alberta moaned, turned, lifted, and brought one full breast to his mouth. He drew it in, tasting its cushy softness as she gasped out little cries.

She pushed her slip and skirt off and his hand moved down to a convex abdomen, slowly sliding across a fleshy waist and finally onto a full, rounded little belly. Yet there was no fat to her, he realized, just a full-fleshed body as opulent as her breasts. Her hands dug into his back as he reached lower, found the very pronounced swell of her pubic mound, a fleshy terrace covered with a rich, black triangle, a soft tuft that sprang up at his touch to curl around his fingers. "Oh, Jeez . . . oh, God," Alberta murmured as he stroked, rubbing and pressing, enjoying the thick denseness of her. Slowly, he let his fingers slide downward again and come in contact with the inner sides of her full-fleshed thighs. He felt their moistness, an imprint of wanting, a lush message of promise, and he felt his own excitement grow. He reached further, to the very end of the hirsute triangle, and touched the sweet, lubricous gateway and Alberta's hips heaved upward as she screamed.

He pressed further, deeper, and her cries rose higher, her legs lifting and opening and closing again around his hand, a fleshy embrace of the senses joining, acting upon each other. He felt her hands pulling on him. "Take me, oh, please, please, take me," she moaned, hurrying words into each other, her legs coming open again. He brought himself over her, pressed down onto her soft groin, and felt her hands pushing forward, searching, finding, closing around his pulsating warmth. Alberta's scream was instant, the sweet victory of sensation that swept aside everything else.

She pulled on him, guided, aided, screamed again, a twisting, spiraling cry as he entered, sliding smoothly into the throbbing tunnel. Alberta's hips rose and twisted, coming to meet his slow thrustings, and her cries matched her every surge. No slow languorousness for Alberta, he saw, as he felt her headlong rush of pleasure carry him along, voluptuous breasts pressed into his face, seeking his mouth, each dark red tip quivering in echo of all of her. "More, more, more," she groaned, and twisting again, she drew back and rushed forward, each movement ascending an invisible ladder of ecstasy until, as she neared the top, her surging thrusts became quick, almost frenzied motions. "Yes, yes, yes, yes, oh, Jeez, yes," Alberta gasped, soft, warm flesh pressed to him, arms and legs encircling him, and he knew he would erupt with her as he saw her head go back and heard the long cry tear from her.

It lingered in the air as she quivered and shook, all the sensual power and pleasure inside her finding itself, ecstasy a volcano of fiery deliverance. Finally, as her cry broke off into something close to a whimper, she fell back but kept his face tight to her breasts. He lay with her sweet smotherings until she pulled her arms away and he let his eyes move across her. Her abdomen was still moving with deep breaths, a faint patina of perspiration covering her luscious body. Slowly, a faint, almost sly smile came to her lips. "Bonus enough?" she murmured.

"Definitely," he said.

"It wasn't just that, Fargo. I told you I've backers who promised to put up towns but I want you to believe in me, in what I'm doing. I know we can work together on a lot of things. I don't know a better way to prove it," she said.

"Can't think of one," Fargo agreed.

"After you finish the third trail I've other things for you," Alberta said.

"More trails?" he inquired.

"Yes, but not around here. You'll have to go north into Washington Territory. That's the one thing that bothers me, sending you off when I want you here with me," she said. "But it'll make your coming back that much sweeter. I'll tell you more after you finish the third trail."

"Good enough," Fargo said and she settled herself into the crook of his arm and was asleep in minutes. He watched her, enjoying the lusciousness of her. Her attitudes reflected her body, direct, forceful, demanding yet pliant. The spirit echoes the flesh, he mused before he closed his eyes and slept beside her until morning. When he rose and washed and finished dressing she had coffee and biscuits waiting for him. She'd thrown on a light nightgown that did little to conceal the ripe allure of her as the opulent breasts swayed with her every movement, pressed into the filmy fabric. Yet there was no immodest show to her, only a frank reveling in her own body, a kind of honesty transmitted by the senses.

Alberta was not only a creature of headlong ambitions but of headlong surprises, he decided and she clung to him when he was ready to leave. "You trying to test my willpower?" he asked.

"No, your remembering," she said.

"No need to test that," he told her. She replied with lips that clung and he left with the feel of her and the taste of her riding with him. When he was beyond the ranch he decided to take the time to pay Willie Baxter a call before going on and turned the horse southwest. It was nearing noon when he drew up at the long cabin, glad to see the mule and horse outside. Willie hurried from the cabin, a skillet in one hand, and Fargo smiled to see the trademark derby on his head.

"Fargo, you're up and around. Good to see that. You're just in time for pancakes," the grizzled figure said.

"Came by to thank you for your visit and your concern," Fargo said. "It was a hairy time, I'll admit."

"And now?"

"Got a last trail to break for Alberta," Fargo said.

"She's going ahead with that crazy plan of hers."

"Very much so, it seems," Fargo said, following Willie into the cabin. He sat down as Willie put the skillet on the stove and poured the batter into it.

"Seems a lot of folks are doing things I don't understand," Willie remarked.

"Such as?"

"Remember I told you there were at least ten outfits who were itching to start operations?" Willie reminded him.

"Yes, but they couldn't because the workforce didn't exist," Fargo recalled.

"That's right. A few such as Sam Bundy with his mining operation, the Greavey brothers and their logging, the Gallardes and their farm, have made use of slave labor. You could add Bart Egan, of course. But the rest have just had to cool their heels. There wasn't a workforce, even with the slave labor on hand. But suddenly they're doing things that say they're expecting to be in operation full steam."

"Who are these outfits?" Fargo questioned as Willie turned his pancakes.

"Ebert and Ebert, a father and son team who want to go into logging equipment. Sam MaComber is out to start a sheep ranch. Rick Dennison plans a big coal mining operation, Frank Dussart a cut lumber plant, and Alex Benjax plans a whiskey distillation operation. Ernie Godge is going to open a tool-making plant and Jake Burns plans a really big hog farm," Willie said.

"All those things are going to take labor, lots of it."

"Damn right. That's why I can't figure it. You don't plan to begin operations until you've got a labor force. You don't put the cart before the horse," Willie said.

"Doesn't make sense," Fargo agreed as he made a mental note of the names Willie had recited. "Maybe they've word that the labor pool is going to widen."

"Then they know something I don't," Willie said as he served the pancakes and produced a jar of sugar pine syrup. "Everything I hear is that there's still a labor shortage in Oregon."

"It doesn't fit, you're right," Fargo said, echoing his own thoughts. "But these pancakes fit. They're mighty fine."

"Think I ought to stick to pancakes, forget anything else," Willie said.

Fargo chewed on Willie's answer as he chewed on the pancakes. "No," he said finally. "You keep your ears open, keep listening. A lot of folks might thank you someday."

"I'll do that. Can't really do anything less. I get uncomfortable when things don't add up," Willie said.

"I understand the feeling," Fargo said as he pushed back and got to his feet. "I've got to move on. Thanks for the pancakes, Willie."

"Glad you're fit again. When do I see you next?" Willie asked.

"I'll stop by soon as I finish this trail for Alberta," Fargo said and Willie waved him away as he rode off, heading east and then south. The things Willie had told him stayed in his thoughts as he rode, but when he could find no explanations that satisfied him he put them aside and concentrated on the trail. He spent the remainder of the day starting to break the third trail, stopping only when night fell, and set out again with daybreak. The land, as it had with the other two trails, resisted his probing with dense underbrush and heavy timber, rugged, twisting terrain that offered false promise time and again. Three days passed before he was able to map a trail that satisfied him and he turned back. He had seen distant land where he could envision farms and other operations taking shape, but he'd seen no place where towns would develop quickly enough to need a stagecoach line.

Nothing had given him more confidence in Alberta's dreams. Except Alberta. He smiled, memory rushing up to tug at him. Making corrections, remarking certain points, redrawing others, he used the next two days to perfect his map and when he reached Alberta's place it was near dusk. He halted in surprise. The house was bathed in light and the sound of laughter and conversation, along with the tinkle of glasses, drifted into the air. The front yard was crowded with horses and carriages, some with drivers lounging beside them. He saw plenty of buckboards, surreys, and light pony wagons and a few slat-bottom road wagons along with a Whitechapel buggy.

Dismounting, he left the Ovaro tethered to the ground and stepped to the door, where women's voices carried over the men's. Alberta opened the door after his third knock, her eyes widening in surprise as she saw him. She wore a deep red gown, bare-shouldered, that showed not only her hazel eyes but the full swell of her breasts. The word came to his lips of itself. "Beautiful," he said. "But I'm afraid I've come at the wrong time."

"Fargo." She smiled. "No, please come in," she said and pulled him by the arm. He stepped into the house, his eyes moving over the room filled with men, most in evening jackets, the women in fancy gowns. "Let me introduce you," she murmured to him. "These are all old friends of my father's." Raising her voice, she spoke to the room as she pulled him forward with her. "This is my special friend, Skye Fargo. I've told a number of you about the trails he's found for me," she began, turning to a somewhat portly man near her. "Sam Gallarde of the famous Gallarde family," she said to Fargo. The next man, taller, with thinning hair and cold eyes, offered a mechanical smile. "Sam MaComber and Mellissa," Alberta said and led Fargo further into the room. "Frank Dussart and Ingrid," she went on. "Rick Dennison and

Sandy, Sam Bundy and Fran." Fargo's eyes narrowed as they met Sam Bundy's bland gaze. "Bill Ebert and Joe Ebert," Alberta went on. "Abe Benjax and Dottie, Jake Burns and Marion, Ernie Godge and Harriet." Fargo nodded to each as he smiled inwardly. None of the women had been introduced as Mrs. and all were at least half the ages of the men. Her last introduction was that of a short, squat figure with a heavy, self-indulgent face who looked uncomfortable in his frock coat. "Bart Egan," she said.

"Glad to meet you, Fargo," Egan boomed out. "I hear you did me a favor." Fargo let one brow lift in question. "You got rid of Big Baldy. He was a problem, always doing things without checking with me, a real problem. I should've turned him out long ago." Fargo allowed a nod as he silently dismissed Bart Egan's little speech, words that were too convenient. Fargo leaned over to take another sweeping glance across the room.

There were a few men she had passed over and he wagered they were the Greavey brothers and Ed Roscom. But everyone in the room had been on the list of names Willie had given him. Coincidence, he asked himself? An accident? Or entirely reasonable? After all, they were all businessmen, entrepreneurs, in the same region. It was likely they'd know one another. Yet he was bothered. Businessmen did not simply get together because they knew each other or were in the same region. They bonded because of a particular element, a cattleman's association, a sheepherder's alliance, a tradesman's union. These men were of vastly different pursuits. What brought them together, he wondered, with their girlfriends in tow. They were plainly celebrating something.

The fact that they were all about to start up their various business ventures? That brought the question Willie had raised. A business without labor couldn't succeed.

Fargo pushed the questions aside until he could find a moment alone with Alberta and as they halted at a side door he whispered to her. "I'm cutting out. I'm not dressed for a swank party," he said.

Her hand tightened on his arm. "But I want to see you," she said. "I expect they'll all be leaving by nine. Come back then. Please?"

"All right," he agreed, aware that decisions were often made for the wrong reasons. The power of low-cut necklines, he muttered to himself as he slipped out the door. Outside, he found night had fallen and he took the Ovaro and rode up a low hill. He halted under a dwarf maple and relaxed where he could see the road below in the distance. He half dozed and came awake when he caught the sound from the road, wagons rolling, the light creak of buckboards and surreys. He waited and gave them all time to go their ways before he rose and rode back to the house. The bright lights had been mostly turned off, he saw, and Alberta answered the door at his knock. She clung to him at once and he enjoyed the soft, warm feel of her.

Finally pulling back, he drew the map from his pocket and gave it to her. "Trail number three finished," he said. She gave a little squeal of delight, pulling him inside and to the sofa, where she took a moment to examine the piece of parchment. Putting the map away, she turned back to him as he watched one creamy breast almost escape the low neckline. But it refused and made its own provocativeness by refusing. "This means I'm finished, too. I can leave and roam about the rest of Oregon," he said.

"And visit little Chinese immigrant girls?" She half pouted.

He shrugged. "A courtesy call," he said.

"Forget it. I told you, I've something else for you," Alberta said.

"Maybe I'd like to just relax," he slid at her.

"You can relax when you come back to me," she said. "This is something else I'm really excited about."

"I'm listening," he said.

"There are a lot of good cattle in Canada that could be brought down through Washington at half the cost of driving herds up here from Texas and southern California. Buyers would go crazy at the prices we could offer. I want you to find a trail from the Canadian border through Washington and down here."

He thought for a moment. It was a plan unencumbered by the wild and unformed dreams she had with her stagecoach line. It was also a chance to visit a territory he'd always wanted to explore. "That'll take a month, maybe more," he said and saw her face fall.

"I know. That's the only thing I don't like, your being away so long. But we'll make up for lost time when you get back," she said.

"More bonuses?" He laughed.

"Bonuses, promises, whatever. I come through. You've learned that," she said.

"My memory's been bad lately," he said blandly.

A tiny smile edged her lips. "We can fix that," she said, and pulling on a snap at her side and the low-cut neckline fell away altogether. Her opulent breasts fairly leaped at him and he caught them with both hands and moments later he lay beside her in the bedroom, letting his eyes enjoy the full, rich body she offered. All the surging desire he'd found last time came again and she filled the night with moans and cries and spirals of ecstasy until she finally lay spent beside him. She fell asleep at once, thoroughly satiated, and he finally closed his eyes, sleeping with her against him until morning came.

She rose with him and fixed breakfast. When he finished dressing, he was surprised to see her clothed, a scarf around her throat. "Looks as if you're going someplace," he said.

"Yes, rushing out this minute. I've an all-day meeting with Bill Braverman, my lawyer. Some things in Father's will, special trusts and funds. Be back in the morning. Will you be here?"

"I can be," he said.

"Good. We've things to talk about before you go to Canada," she said.

"Did I agree to go?" he asked.

"I thought so. Maybe I misunderstood last night," she said a little reproachfully.

"I guess not." He smiled and saw the smug little grin cross her face as she hurried out. The questions he wanted to ask about the party would wait, he told himself and finished his coffee. When he rode from the ranch he glanced at a dozen hands at the bunkhouses, one of the mountain wagons still there filled with lumber and tools. He rode on, letting himself wander as Alberta's party still lay in his thoughts and, perhaps a subconscious result, he found himself at Willie Baxter's long cabin. Willie hurried out to greet him.

"This must mean you finished that last trail for the Foster girl," Willie said.

"She's got more plans for me," Fargo said as he dismounted and went into the cabin with Willie. There were tools spread out on the floor. "I come at a bad time?" he asked.

"No. The Crawleys, they're east of here, want me to fix their old stove. I'm just picking out the tools to take," Willie said. "I was on the road yesterday afternoon, saw Sam MaComber and Bart Egan in a surrey, all dressed up, couple of girls with them."

"They were on their way to a party at Alberta's," Fargo said. "I stopped in, met everybody on that list you gave me." Willie's eyes widened and Fargo told him about the party and those there.

"What kind of party?" Willie asked.

"Never did find that out. But I will. Maybe they were all celebrating starting up their various ventures," Fargo said.

"Without labor. Still can't figure out that," Willie said.

"Been thinking about that. Maybe they know there's a labor force on the way," Fargo said and Willie frowned back. "Mr. Han got a letter from China telling him that three boatloads of new immigrants are on their way here. Three boatloads will bring a good lot of workers."

"They would." Willie nodded. "But how'd they know about it here?"

"The people in the village know about the letter. Some who work for good, honest employers such as Ryan could have talked and it got around to the likes of the

Greavey Brothers, Sam Bundy, Bart Egan. They'd spread the word to others, for sure," Fargo said.

"They would," Willie said and he frowned hard into space for so long that Fargo broke into his thoughts.

"What are you thinking?" Fargo inquired.

"Something a lot worse," Willie said. "About the shipwreck of the Portuguese trader that turned out to be a slave ship, the one the little Chinese girl was on."

"What about it?"

"What if the three boatloads on their way here are going to be more of the same?" Willie said. "Maybe that's why our friends are so sure they'll be getting a labor force, not because they overheard talk but because they've paid the Portuguese captains and crew."

Fargo felt the shock of Willie's words go through him, the enormity of it chilling, too horrible to consider yet all too possible. Was the shipwrecked Portuguese trader more than he had imagined, no single, isolated instance but the forerunner of a paid program for human degradation? He felt sickened at the thought and made himself remember that it was still all speculation, conjecture, sound without substance. Yet if it were true, if Willie had hit on a terrible truth, where did Alberta fit? She'd hosted a party for all of them? Why? What was it for? What was her role?

Those answers could change speculation into fact. If in fact, Alberta did have answers, he pondered. He had no trouble seeing her as that creature of wild, impractical dreams. Everything she had done affirmed that, from explanations to ecstasy. But perhaps she knew things without knowing she did. That could happen, he knew. He'd find out, he promised himself. Willie's voice broke into his thoughts. "You're thinking about her," Willie said.

"You're getting too sharp," Fargo said. "I won't jump to conclusions about her. If what we're thinking is right, that doesn't mean she's involved. They could be using her in some way."

"I won't rule that out," Willie said. It was a gesture of fairness, considering how he felt about her father. Fargo accepted it appreciatively.

"I'll talk to her tomorrow. She may know a lot or nothing at all. I'll let you know," he said. Willie nodded and stayed in the doorway as Fargo left. As he rode the Ovaro up the road at a walk, the sun began lowering over the hills, but he kept a slow walk. He wanted to be near Alberta's place in the morning to pay an early visit. When night came he felt he was close enough and bedded down in a clump of serviceberry. He filled his mind with positive thoughts about Alberta, relived the nights he'd lain with her. It made going to sleep easier.

6

The morning dawned hot and humid and when he rode into Alberta's place he saw her horse being stabled by one of the hands. She greeted him at the door with a kiss and a hug and looked very awake; her alert, hazel eyes searching his face. "You're looking very serious this morning," she said.

"Some mornings come up that way," he said. "A lot of questions keep poking at me."

"Such as?" she asked.

"Your party," he said. "Some of the people you had there. Sam Bundy, Bart Egan, the Greavey brothers. Some others, too."

She fastened a small frown on him. "You been talking to old men with delusions again," she said.

"Some, but I found out enough on my own. What were you doing giving a party with the likes of Sam Bundy and Bart Egan there, or the Gallardes and the Greavey brothers? They're vicious, no-good slave labor users," Fargo said.

"And they were all friends of my father's," Alberta answered. "It was a kind of memorial. They all wanted it and I went along with that."

"Memorial? Seemed more like a celebration, all with girlfriends on hand," Fargo said.

She gave a half shrug. "Celebration, memorial, they're not all that different," Alberta said. "It was a good time with lots of good memories of my father."

Fargo made no comment but he thought of how Willie would put it: memories shared by cheats, liars, and thieves about another cheat, liar, and thief. But even if Willie was right about Albert Madison Foster, and everything else they'd speculated upon, that didn't condemn Alberta and he peered at her for a long moment. "I want to believe you, that that's all it was, a kind of memorial," Fargo said.

"What else would it be for?" Alberta said, her hazel eyes wide. "I'm not ready to throw a party for my new stagecoach line yet."

"No, you're not," he said, deciding not to share the thoughts he and Willie had explored. Perhaps the less she knew the better off she'd be, he reasoned, yet he felt slightly traitorous. She'd given all of herself so he'd believe in her. He owed that much to her. Yet he stayed silent as her arms came around his neck, her pliant lips pressing his mouth.

"You try to do the best you can with what you've inherited. That includes people as well as things. I didn't pick and choose all of Father's friends," she murmured.

"No, of course not," he muttered and felt very small.

"Think whatever you want about them. Just believe in me," she said, stepping back and leading him into her bedroom. "You have anything against fun in the morning?" she asked.

"No," he said and began to unbutton his shirt as she

did her blouse. She came to him with a new urgency, a tremendous explosion of desire until, under the noon sun, she lay gasping beside him, opulent breasts rising and falling with her every deep, satisfied breath.

Later, when he was dressed and she'd donned a robe, she held him a moment more. "When can you leave for Canada?" she asked.

"Tomorrow?" he said. "Maybe the day after."

"Whatever gives us another night together," she said. "You satisfied about the party?" He nodded as he held her. "Not everything is complex. Some things are simply explained," she said. He agreed silently, glad for simple explanations he could embrace.

When he left, he started to go toward Willie Baxter's cabin. But he changed his mind, reversed his steps, and instead went onto the trail he had mapped out to the coast. He'd give Willie Alberta's simple explanation of the party. He had no trouble with his own acceptance but he knew Willie would be a good deal more cynical. A little concrete evidence of how Alberta was moving forward with her own plans would let him accept her explanations more readily. It'd show she had her own agenda, not involved with any of the others, her own dreams no matter how impractical they were.

He put the Ovaro into a nice, easy trot and refused to even consider that blaming Willie's cynicism could hide his own. He enjoyed following the trail he had mapped but night fell before he reached the spot where he'd seen the way station being erected. He bedded down and slept until morning when he went on again. When he reached the straight stretch of trail, he slowed, his eyes on the way station. It was finished, he saw, roof on, all the sides and windows in place, two doors at either end. It still re-sembled a barracks more than a way station, he thought as he rode to a halt beside it. The workmen had left a hammer and a saw, he noted as he walked to the door, pulled it open, and went inside. The frown slid across his brow, growing deeper as he swept the interior of the structure with a long stare.

Rows of bunk beds filled one large room, one over the other. It was no way station with rooms for travelers to sleep, women to undress and change. He explored, and saw nothing even resembling a kitchen. "A damn bar-racks," he muttered aloud, stepped outside, and saw where a row of outhouses had been placed. He paused for another survey of the interior of the structure and then climbed onto the Ovaro. A cascade of dark thoughts swept through him as he rode and he knew he was un-willing to pursue most of them, yet he could not shut them out. They danced inside him, mocking and offering explanations he refused to entertain yet could not push away. He was on his way to Willie's cabin by the time night fell and he knew that now he'd welcome the old man's cynicism. He couldn't find explanations fighting with his own demons. He needed someone to throw back fears and faith, and reinforce believing or betrayal. Doing it alone was too hard. It let one turn aside, it let one alone to believe or to condemn, both too easy to do.

The light was on in the cabin when he rode up. Willie heard the hoofbeats and came to the door, the big, old Walken in his hands. "You're full of surprises, old friend," Willie said as he lowered the rifle. "Drink?" he asked as Fargo followed him into the cabin.

"Damn right," Fargo said, flinging himself into a chair.

"You look like a man that's real bothered," Willie said, bringing a bottle of good, rye, sipping whiskey. "You didn't get the answers you wanted from Alberta?"

"I got a fine answer from her, a simple explanation that fitted real well," Fargo said.

"Then what's the trouble?" Willie questioned.

"It's easy to run off with the bit, that's what the trouble is," Fargo snapped angrily.

"It is," Willie agreed. "I'm listening." Fargo grunted as he took a deep draw of the whiskey and began by telling him everything Alberta had explained to him, the answer she'd given, and how he'd believed her.

"She even said you do the best you can with what you've inherited. You don't pick and choose your pa's friends and she's right," Fargo said and heard the defensiveness in his voice. He hurried on to tell Willie about the way station that was really a barracks, a big bunkhouse and how the sight of it had triggered a deluge of dark thoughts he was ashamed to harbor.

Willie thought in silence when he finished, plainly going over everything Fargo had said. "You're really wondering about that last thing she said to you," Willie submitted slowly. "You do the best you can with what you've inherited, she said. You're not really wondering about the friends she inherited. You're wondering whether she's inherited good blood or bad. Is she made to live a good and honorable life or to follow her pa and lie, steal, and murder? That's what you're really wondering, boy."

"I guess so," Fargo conceded grimly. "And on a practical level I'm wondering about ships arriving and way stations that are really barracks and trails that don't really go anywhere."

"Let's look at the possibilities. Slave labor unloaded from ships are taken on the trail you mapped out. But they can't go all the way across the state without a place to rest, a halfway stopping place. Is the way station really just that?"

"And does Alberta know it? Or has she been taken in, sold a bill of goods by people smarter and nastier?" Fargo said.

"How do you figure to find that out?" Willie queried.

"Ask," Fargo snapped. "But hard questions, this time, with no sweet talk, smooth answers."

"What if she's being used? What then?" Willie followed.

"Find a way to stop them," Fargo said. "But that'll take some thinking and some doing."

"Count me in," Willie said as Fargo nodded and rose, his lips a thin line. The visit with Willie hadn't made anything easier, just a little more defined and that gave him an added resolution he was grateful to have. Willie waved good-bye when he left and made his way through the night after declining the offer of shelter. Fargo wanted to retrace his steps and be closer to Alberta's place before the next day drew late. He bedded down alongside the road, back in a cluster of white alder. His whirling thoughts kept sleep at bay, most all of them centered around Alberta.

He had believed her explanation for the party. She had seen to that, he recalled. But he wanted to keep believing her, he admitted to himself. Weren't we supposed to trust, to have faith, he asked and knew that was but one more question without a clear answer. Grimacing, he set aside his whirling thoughts and drew sleep around himself, finally succumbing to the still of the night. The morning woke him early and he found a cluster of hackberry and feasted on the sugary, thin pulp of the drupes, washing everything down with the cold, clear water of a stream.

He arranged his thoughts, wanting his questions all in place when he faced Alberta. It was late afternoon when he reached her place, reining to a halt before he entered. A two-seat fringed-top surrey with a brace of bays waited outside the door and Fargo turned the pinto, moving back and slipping into a line of black cottonwoods that stretched around the side of the house. Staying in the trees, he moved opposite the house, dismounting and leaning against the deeply furrowed bark. He waited as the day drifted into night and lamps went on in the house. In the bunkhouse, too, he saw. An hour went by, then another, and the bunkhouse lamps began to go out one by one. But the surrey still stayed outside the main house until suddenly, the door opened and Fargo straightened to peer at the stream of light that came from the doorway. Alberta came out, the Greavey brothers with her. Behind them Frank Dussart and Ernie Godge followed, the men all climbing into the surrey with Frank Dussart taking the reins.

Good-byes and waves were exchanged, the surrey drove off, and Alberta went into the house. The furrow digging into his brow growing deeper, Fargo waited till the surrey was well out of sight before crossing to the house in a dozen silent strides. He thought of entering without knocking, but decided against it, and rapped softly. The door opened, Alberta's eyes widening. "Fargo. You're made of surprises," she said and he noted how her dress clung to every full curve of her.

"You, too," he said gruffly and stepping inside, he pushed the door shut behind him. "I'm made of questions, too," he added.

A quizzical little furrow touched her forehead. "More questions?" she asked with a deprecating little smile.

"More," he said. "We'll start with way stations. I want to know why yours is really a damn bunkhouse full of double bunks."

The furrow on her forehead became a frown. "I don't know," she answered.

"Try again. Wrong answer," he snapped. "Not good enough."

"It'll have to be," she said, her face stiffening. "I'd nothing to do with the building of it. I haven't even seen it. They told me they'd take care of building the way station after I had a trail."

"Who's they?" Fargo pushed at her.

"My backers. I told you I had investors. Bill and Joe Ebert are among them. They built the station. I don't know what they put up or why," Alberta answered.

He turned the answer over in his mind, and grimaced inwardly. It was entirely plausible and she had mentioned backers. But he'd promised himself not to accept simple answers. "You still don't have a stagecoach. You said you'd have one by now. Did I map a trail for something else?" he pressed.

"For what? I don't understand what you're talking about," Alberta threw back. "I expected my Concord by now. I can't help that they didn't deliver." Resentment darkened her eyes as she glared at him and he grimaced inwardly. Once again, it was an entirely plausible answer. "Why all these questions? What's all this about?" She pushed at him, her voice rising.

"It's about things that don't fit right, things that cast strange shadows," he said.

"Such as?" she challenged.

"Such as your friends just now, men who use slave labor and others who are desperate to find workers. Your father's friends, you told me. That's why you had the party, because they wanted a memorial affair. What were they doing here tonight? Planning another memorial?" he flung at her and saw her eyes darken at his sarcasm.

"The Greavey brothers have backed me, just as the Eberts did. Dussart and Godge want in. They want to invest in my stageline. That's what they came to talk about, what they could offer, what I'd agree to, financial and practical details. They've confidence in my ideas, unlike some people I know," she said and he heard the hurt in her voice. "You're not just made of questions, you're made of suspicions," she said, sadness joining the hurt. He swore silently. "I think perhaps you should leave now," she said.

"Good idea," he said, wanting to get out, to be alone to think. There were no more questions he'd ask and he'd tell nothing more. She'd given her explanations and he wanted to digest them. He reached the door when she called out.

"You're being unfair, you know," she said, sounding terribly hurt again.

"I need thinking time," he said, opening the door. "I'll be back tomorrow."

"One thing," she called and he paused, not turning. "Be ready to leave for Canada. This doesn't change anything, not for me. I won't be childish."

He swore inwardly. She was being noble, damn her, showing him she could rise above being hurt. "Tomorrow," he growled and stalked from the house, the door slamming shut behind him. He strode into the trees, swung onto the pinto, and rode into the open as he left the ranch. But he didn't ride far, just enough to be beyond the ranch and pull beneath a wide-branched broadleaf maple from where he could see the house. Thoughts whirled through his head in a wild circle, chasing one another with maddening inconsistency.

Her explanations had all been couched in reason and plausibility. It was easy to see her as being used, to understand her not questioning those who offered to help her, not suspecting motives. It was normal that she eagerly accept those who supported her impractical dreams. She'd drawn a picture of herself as trusting, accepting, almost naïve. He knew he wanted to believe that picture, yet little things kept holding him back. Alberta said she'd accepted the Eberts' offer to build the way station and hadn't even seen it yet. But he remembered how she'd examined every detail of the maps he'd drawn with concentrated attention. It was difficult to believe she hadn't done the same with the plans for the Eberts' way station, or gone to look at it.

She had agreed to have the Greavey brothers as backers. They were old friends of her father's, she said as a reason. Yet she had to know they were slave labor users. She'd dismissed the accusation as exaggeration. And he remembered her remarks about Mei Ling. They were neither accepting nor understanding. They'd been icy and uncaring. Because she was jealous, she had said. He had to wonder if that was enough of a reason, as he realized she was still a question mark. One he wanted to believe, he admitted angrily. He waited for the lights to go out in the house. Finally, they did, except for a lone candle left burning in one window.

He was about to turn away when the door opened and Alberta came out. She had changed to jodhpurs and a white shirt. She strode to the barn, emerged minutes later on her horse, and passed him only a dozen yards away as she rode into the night at a fast trot. He frowned after her as she disappeared from sight, thought about following, and decided against it. He could always pick up her tracks come dawn. Instead, he moved the pinto toward the house, tethered the horse around the back, and hurried to the front door, opened it, and went inside. The candle in the window afforded enough glow for him to make his way past the living room, and he saw the small study on the other side of the bedroom. He stepped into the room, found the small kerosene lamp, and turned it on. The light spread across a wooden desk, manila envelopes and a file box on the desk along with pen and inkstand. A number of three-by-four index cards were scattered on the table where Alberta had plainly been working with them.

He sat down, opened the file box, and saw more of the file cards neatly in place, each with words and figures written on them. He took out the cards and as he began to examine them, he felt the frown slide across his brow. The first card bore the name Sam Bundy. Beside it there was an address and underneath it the number sixty. Next to the number were the letters *M* only. He went to the next card. It carried the name Greavey Brothers, the address, and beneath it the number forty. Next to the number he read *M* only. He went to the next card. It carried the name Gallarde family and the number thirty-five. Next to the number, he read *M* and *F*. Poring through each of the cards, Fargo found the names of every one of those who had been at Alberta's party, Ebert and Ebert, Sam MaComber, Rick Dennison, Frank Dussart, and all the others. Beside each name was a number ranging from ten to sixty. Beside Bart Egan's name he saw the number ten and the letter *F* only.

He sat back, stared at the little cards, the meaning of each rising up before his eyes, each an order specifying how many workers were wanted and how many of each sex. They were a terrible, human shopping list and he felt sick inside. They all lay on her desk, throbbing with a malignant life of their own, all turning Willie's questions and conjectures into wrenching fact, all forming a blueprint of ruthless, selfish disregard for human life. The arrangements for bringing in the labor force needed had all been made, carefully prepared. But they still needed one thing, a trail they could use to transport their human cargo, a trail they hadn't been able to find. That's when Alberta had called him in, Fargo muttered to himself, his eyes narrowed, to give them the last thing they didn't have.

Everything she'd told him had been a story woven around that. Even the trip to Canada, he realized now. It was designed to keep him away when the boats arrived. All the rest of her elaborate story had been a concoction, impractical dreams, a fairy tale of the imagination. The human shopping list staring back at him had torn apart the very heart of belief and trust, given the lie to every smooth explanation. Soft thighs had been soft lies, ecstasy used to deceive. Perhaps that was the hardest of all to take.

Getting to his feet, he put the cards back in the file box, turned the lamp out, and crossed the darkened living room to the door. Pulling the door open, he halted, cursing softly as he stared at the six rifles facing him in a semicircle. His eyes went to the men behind the guns, then to the open door of the bunkhouse in the distance. One man, thin, with a lean face, a narrow nose, and straggly long hair, growled the single word. "Surprise," he said.

Fargo's lips pursed and he nodded in agreement. They'd plainly been waiting. "How'd you know?" he asked.

"We take turns checking the place through the night, saw the candle in the window and checked the barn, saw her horse was gone. Miss Foster left in a hurry. She doesn't usually leave a candle on. We checked the house, saw the lamplight," the man said and Fargo swore inwardly. "Drop your gun, slow and easy," the thin one ordered. Fargo eyed the odds, grimaced, and carefully obeyed. The six rifles couldn't miss at this range. One of the men picked up the Colt and the others seized him and Fargo watched the men hand the Colt to the thin one, who pushed it into his belt.

"We hold him till she gets back?" one of the men asked.

"No. We'll take him to the Greaveys'. They pay us, not her," the narrow-faced one said and Fargo had a moment's surprise at the remark. But it added one more link between Alberta and those who traded in slave labor. "Get him on his horse. We'll take him now," the thin one said.

Fargo's thoughts raced. The thin throwing knife was in his calf holster and he wanted time and opportunity to use it. He'd get both put in a room alone to wait. "Alberta won't like that," he spoke up. "She'll have questions for me."

"I don't give a shit what she'd like. I answer to the Greaveys," the thin one snarled. Fargo fell silent as one of the others brought the Ovaro and he climbed onto the horse with three six-guns trained on him. The six men brought their horses as Fargo saw there were other hands watching from the bunkhouse. Watching carefully, Fargo waited as the six riders surrounded him, one on each side of him, the thin one in front of him with another man and two riders behind. Any move for the calf holster would surely be seen, first by the two at his back. He moved off with the six guards, into the dark night and the rugged terrain beyond the ranch. Thoughts whirled through his mind as he rode but he found himself discarding one after another, and as time marched on he felt the edge of desperation pushing at him.

It'd be daylight in another few hours and his chances for making a break would mostly evaporate. They had gone another hour when they began to climb a steep hillside heavily timbered with mountain ash. Making their way carefully along uneven ground and thick trees, the six riders moved him along with them. But the steep terrain exacted a price, Fargo noted. The thin man in front had moved ahead of his companion. A quick glance showed that the two riders behind him had fallen back a dozen feet, their horses struggling with the climb. One of the riders at his side had moved away as he negotiated his way around a thick tree trunk. The other was still close beside him.

Fargo felt his body tighten. It was probably the only moment he'd have, Fargo decided. The only drawback was the fact that everyone was a shadowy, indistinct figure in the dark and the trees. But he couldn't wait and hope for another chance that might never present itself. Pushing up from the stirrups, he flung himself sideways, slammed into the rider alongside him, and went down with his arms wrapped around the man. They hit the ground together, Fargo on top, and he heard the man's head hit the ground, his body go limp as he fell into unconsciousness. Passing up the knife in his calf holster, Fargo yanked the man's six-gun from its holster as the shouts of alarm erupted.

Rolling, Fargo fired from on his back, caught one of the two men who'd been riding behind him and the figure pitched forward from his horse. But the others had time to recover from their initial surprise and wheel their horses, he knew. Rolling again, he dived into a thicket of underbrush just as the barrage of shots hurtled into where he'd been. He saw the body of the unconscious man he'd knocked from the saddle shudder as the bullets thudded into him. Finding one of the shadowy figures, Fargo fired again and the man cried out as he spun, went down, and was silent. Fargo lay flat and heard the others break cover and leap from their horses. He pushed backward behind a tree and gathered his thoughts. There were three left. That was their advantage. They outnumbered him three to one. They only needed one of them to get off a lucky shot.

But he had an advantage, too. They were ordinary ranch hands. They weren't trailsmen. They didn't know how to listen. They didn't know how to move through the woods. They didn't know the ways of silence. They couldn't hunt, not beast nor man. They lacked the knowing and the discipline. That was his advantage, Fargo knew, and he lay silent, gathered his self-discipline, and waited. He hardly breathed, his ears fine-tuned to the tiniest sound and its meaning. He hadn't all that long to wait and he grunted with a grim satisfaction. The first sounds he picked up were the whispers, barely audible, ending as abruptly as they had begun.

Fargo lay still and listened to the rustle of grass and leaves. But not rustled by footsteps, by bodies crawling forward on their bellies. He almost smiled. They crawled not as silent serpents but as groundhogs, amateurs at stealth. He raised the revolver as he lay flat, peering through the darkness, still listening to sounds. They were inching their way separated by a half-dozen feet, their plan to find him, then pour bullets at him from three directions. His ears acted as eyes, tracing their approach as they slithered down the hill, moving past trees. The one in the center edged a little ahead of the other two, Fargo's ears told him, and he shifted the six-gun to his right. The sound suddenly ceased. They had halted to listen. Fargo let them listen to absolute silence and in a few moments, they inched forward again.

The hillside spread up just above where he lay and Fargo's eyes slowly moved back and forth across the slope when suddenly they halted. A shape came into sight, crawling past the base of a young ash. It was the figure in the center, the two others materializing a half-dozen feet behind. Almost directly in front of him, the crawling figure moved closer and Fargo glanced again at the other two figures. All had their guns out, he was certain. They'd be able to fire at once and they'd do so the minute he fired. But it'd take them a half second to zero in on where his shot had come from.

He gathered his strength and counted off seconds. He had but three shots left in the borrowed six-gun and he couldn't count on the weapon being as accurate as his Colt. Timing and marksmanship would spell success or failure, and he could be certain only of one kill. His lips pulled back in a grimace. He couldn't afford to let them come down any closer. The closer they came the faster the other two could get off their shots. He took aim, slowly pressed the trigger of the six-gun, and the single shot split the darkness. He had only a fleeting moment to see the dark spray of liquid arc into the air in all directions, the silent fountain terrible proof that he had not missed.

He flung himself into a roll and came up onto his stomach as the shots exploded from the other two figures, four in all, fired at where he had been. His first answering shot caught the second figure and he heard the man's gargled gasp and saw him half rise only to collapse in an inert mound. The last man pushed to his feet, spun, and tried to half run and half crawl up the slope. Fargo's final bullet caught him as he reached a tree to hide behind. He pitched forward, his hands clasping the bark of the tree as he slowly slid downward and lie still. Fargo paused another moment, then rose and walked to the first figure, but found he was able to recognize only the man's long, straggly hair. But he saw what he'd come to find—his Colt sticking in the man's belt—and he retrieved the gun, dropped it into his holster, and gave a low whistle.

The Ovaro appeared from up on the slope and carefully made its way down. Fargo swung onto the horse. He kept it going downhill until he reached the end of the slope, turning left and riding back toward Alberta's place. The dawn was just beginning to touch the sky when he reached the ranch, moving along the road until he found what he sought—the hoofprints of a single horse moving fast, those of Alberta's mount as she rode off in the night. He followed as the dawn rose, saw the prints turn in a half circle and go east. He continued to follow, slowing as he saw the land open up and the collection of buildings appear at the edge of a river where hundreds of logs floated against one another.

The tall timber had turned to mostly Sitka spruce, Douglas fir, and ponderosa pine, he noted. One house, larger and more imposing than the others, sat back from the river. He saw a number of surreys, buckboards, and mountain wagons in the front yard of the main house. He also saw Alberta's horse tied there. He took a moment to scan the main camp, saw the heavy, wide-wheeled logging rigs and at least twenty loggers with their distinctive belts doing various chores, some with long poles balancing themselves on logs in the water. The sun told him it was midafternoon and he moved the Ovaro behind a line of Sitka spruce as he rode closer. He didn't need the small sign that told him he was at the Greavey brothers' logging camp as, staying inside the spruce, he drew closer to the main house.

From the wagons outside the house, it was plain there was some sort of conference going on inside and he wanted to hear whatever he could. There were too many eyes that would see him at the front door so he moved the Ovaro through the spruce until he reached the rear of the house. Dropping the reins over a low branch, he stepped to the edge of the trees, peered across the short open space to the house, checked both corners, and darted forward to the rear door. It opened at his touch and he slipped into the house, into a rear vestibule. From the kitchen to one side he could hear the murmur of voices from the front of the house. Creeping silently, he passed two rooms of the large house and the voices grew louder, words distinct now, and he glimpsed a large living room, figures seated and standing inside.

He dropped low and crept to the edge of the doorway that let him see into the room. He found Alberta first, seated in a stuffed chair, arms behind her, and alongside her he saw Bart Egan and Sam Bundy beside him. He swept the room with a quick glance, and saw the Eberts, the Gallardes, Rick Dennison, and just about everyone else.

Ed Greavey, standing, held the floor as the others listened. "Then it's settled," Fargo heard Ed Greavey say. "You all know what you're to do."

"I've ten men ready and waiting," Joe Ebert said.

"I've a dozen standing by," one of the Gallardes said.

"Six," Rick Dennison put in.

"Eight," Frank Dussart said and so it went around the room, each supplying a number. When they finished they had counted off some sixty men.

"Good. We'll have enough armed men to handle everyone we take off the boats," Greavey said. "We've two lookouts on the shore now, round the clock. Soon as the first boat drops anchor one of the lookouts will ride like hell to me. I'll get word to the rest of you. Get your men there right away. We want to start moving them soon as we can."

"What about the ones nobody wants?" Dennison asked.

"The ocean's right there," Sam Bundy answered.

Fargo's stomach turned, first at the mercilessness of Sam Bundy's words, second at the fact that he had helped them perfect their ruthless plan—his trails were the avenues they'd use. His eyes held on Alberta. She sat unmoving, her face expressionless and he cursed silently at her.

"Get back to your places and wait. It won't be long. The boats are overdue now," Greavey said, and Fargo watched them start to leave, all except Alberta, who stayed seated. Dussart and Bundy halted, gestured to Alberta.

"What about her?" Bundy asked.

"She'll stay here with me," Greavey said. "Her part's finished." Dussart and Bundy left and three of Greavey's loggers entered the room. Greavey nodded at Alberta and she rose. The three men started from the room with her and Fargo felt his eyes grow wide as he stared at Alberta. Her hands were tied behind her back. "Put her in the cellar," Greavey ordered.

"Bastards, all of you," Alberta flung back as she was led from the room. Fargo's eyes were so wide they hurt and he continued to stare after Alberta when she was gone. Her bound wrists blazed into his mind. She was their prisoner. The fact repeated itself and did it again. It defied belief as it demanded no less. He stayed frozen in place, unable to move, unable to think of anything else, enveloped in total shock.

7

Only the three men returning to the room snapped the shock that had seized him in a grip of its own. "Got her tied?" Greavey asked and the men nodded. Fargo began to move backward on silent steps, and reached the rear door as Greavey and his men left the room. But even shock did not let the caution that was part of him slip away. He edged the door open, peered outside, and making certain no one was in sight, silently closed the door and streaked for the spruce. He dove into their protective green cloak where the Ovaro waited. Dropping to one knee, he drew in a long, deep breath.

Only one scene filled his mind, replaying itself as only one fact screamed at him. She had been their prisoner, not an ally, a prisoner. The impact of it shattered every conclusion he had made in Alberta's study in front of the index cards. What had been proof was suddenly no proof at all. What had drawn itself crystal clear was now cloaked in murk and mud. Questions speared into him. Had he somehow misread everything he'd discovered? That seemed impossible and it in fact was impossible. They were waiting for the ships. They intended to take them across the trails he'd found for them, to use the mock way station they'd built. He'd not been wrong about that. But had he been monumentally wrong about Alberta's involvement? Had he completely misread her role? If he had, it was, in its own way, the one bright spot in the terrible picture that had revealed itself.

He had to know. That was the first thing he had to do and his eyes peered through the trees. Dusk had begun to push away the day. He'd wait and find a way to free Alberta. He settled down to watch night take over the land. The loggers streamed to their bunkhouses and lights went on in the main house. The logging camp eventually grew still and finally the lamplight went out in the main house. Fargo crept carefully from the trees and once more made his way to the rear of the house, where he slipped inside. An oil lamp in a hallway afforded a dim light and he halted and listened, before he went further into the house. But he heard only silence. He crept down a long hallway and came upon a door as he neared the front of the house. He tried the knob. It turned, the door opening, and he saw the flight of steps that led downward.

He started down, taking each step one at a time, testing each to make sure it didn't groan before he put weight on it. As he reached the bottom of the steps he saw the small candle that gave off a flickering light inside a large basement. Most of the room held trunks and boxes and then he saw the cot at the far end, almost hidden by a stack of boxes. He crossed the floor and the flickering light outlined Alberta's figure on the cot. He saw the ropes that tied her hands and ankles to the underside of the cot so she had room to turn on her side but not much more.

She was asleep and he placed one hand over her mouth. She snapped awake, her eyes frightened. He let her take a moment to recognize him and then withdrew his hand. "Oh, God, Fargo," she breathed, watching as he began to untie the ropes that bound her to the metal frame under the cot. "Can't you cut them? It'll be quicker," she asked.

"Then they'll know somebody freed you. I don't want that," Fargo said. "This way they'll think you somehow untied yourself." She nodded and fell silent as he worked on the ropes until he had untied each. She sat up and flung her arms around him, clinging for a moment.

"How'd you know I was here?" she murmured.

"We'll talk later. My questions, first," he said. She nodded, stood up with him, and stayed a half step behind him as he started up the stairway. There was only silence at the top and he led her down the hallway and out the rear door. "Stay against the house and see if your horse is still there. If it is, walk to the spruce," he said, and crossed to the trees and waited. She materialized a few moments later, leading the horse, and when she reached the trees he took to the saddle and led the way through the spruce. Not until they were well away from the logging camp did he stop and swing from the saddle. She dismounted as well.

He faced her with his jaw set, the muscles in his face throbbing. "I was at your place. I'd put most of it together already. The index cards finished the picture. Now talk, dammit, the truth for a change. You brought me in. You were part of it."

She stared back and he watched her beautifully patrician face pulling thoughts together. "I know what it must look like to you," she said.

"It looks like what it was, goddammit," he shot back. "You lying to me all along. You making up all sorts of stories to cover up what you and the others were really planning."

"That's true," she said and the moment of surprise stabbed at him, took him aback. But his fury asserted itself at once.

"Confession may be good for the soul but it doesn't change anything," he threw at her.

"I know that," she said softly. He stared at her and swore silently at her contrition because he still wanted to find a way to believe in her.

"I just want to know why they had you tied up," he said.

"Because it's not what you're thinking. It never was," Alberta said.

"Hell it wasn't," Fargo snapped.

"Not for me. They found that out."

"Found what out?" he demanded.

Her lips pursed. "That I was only pretending to be a part of their plan," Alberta said evenly. "I was working with Sheriff Yancey." Fargo heard his own breath draw in a sharp gasp. "They had combined in a group to use slave labor and others were joining in. The sheriff suspected this but he'd no proof. He decided the only way he could stop them was to get the kind of proof only someone on the inside could get. He talked about it with me and I decided to do it. I became part of their plans. It wasn't hard, seeing as how they'd been old friends of my father's. They took me in easily."

"All the stories you made up for me was part of the plan," Fargo said.

"That's right." Alberta nodded. "Bringing you in helped get the things they needed such as the trails but it also added more of the proof the sheriff needs." Her arms came up, encircling his neck. "I couldn't tell you. I couldn't tell anyone. The sheriff and I agreed that was the only really safe way to go. I was putting the finishing touches on getting the final proof when you became suspicious. You could say it was a case of you being too smart."

"How did they find out about you?" Fargo asked.

She frowned in thought for a moment. "I don't know. I've no idea. But when I went to the Greaveys' place they grabbed me. They knew. I'm sure they intended to kill me in another day if you hadn't come along." Her lips found his and he felt as though a terrible weight had been lifted from him. He'd not been wrong believing in her and that was a good feeling, even better than the satisfaction of having seen through the scheme. When her lips finally pulled from his he gave her a hand onto her horse and climbed onto the pinto.

"Let's go," he said.

"Where?" Alberta asked.

"You can't go to your place. They might go looking there. I know a place for you. Then I've a lot to do and damn little time to do it." He put the pinto into a canter, stayed in it, and rode in silence as plans formed inside him. A new day had come before he reached the long cabin. Willie came out, surprise flooding his eyes as they found Alberta. Fargo dismounted and spoke quickly, told Willie all he'd found out, and ended with everything Alberta had confessed to him.

"Lots of twists and turns to that story," Willie murmured. "But seems it came out right and that's what counts."

"You two can get to be friends in time," Fargo said. "Meanwhile, I'd like Alberta to stay here, Willie. It's the only safe place I know. They won't think of looking for her here."

"Whatever you want, Fargo," Willie said, turning to Alberta. "The second room's yours. There are extra work clothes inside if you want."

"Thank you, Willie," Alberta said softly and went into the cabin as Fargo took Willie aside.

"Been thinking this out as best I can," Fargo said, keeping his voice low with Willie. "None of it comes out good but I've got to get those people off the boats before Greavey and the others get to them. That's the first order of business. I don't get them off first they wind up slave labor."

"Off to where?" Willie questioned.

"Han Village, it's the only place," Fargo said.

"You think the others will just back off after all this? Everything they need depends on that slave labor," Willie reminded him.

"Maybe they won't. I want to give those in the village a chance to fight, to protect themselves. I'll need you for that. Can you get a hundred rifles in town?" Fargo asked.

"A hundred rifles?" Willie frowned. "Maybe a dozen. You need a gun dealer for a hundred rifles."

Fargo grimaced, the answer one he had unhappily expected. "How about dynamite sticks?" he asked. "I know it's new but it's being used."

"Yep, been using it myself. It's a lot safer than nitro-glycerin. Dick Enders sells dynamite sticks to miners, loggers, prospectors. I can get you all you want. I've some here myself."

"How many?" Fargo inquired quickly.

"I've probably got a half-dozen out back," Willie said.

"I'll take them. But I want you to get another fifty sticks. When you get them, take them to Han Village and show them how to use them."

"I light them with lucifers," Willie said.

"You show them," Fargo said. "But I want you to go to the village now and bring Mei Ling back. I'll need her. Ask her if she can bring two more of her people with her. I'll wait for you where the trail I mapped to the coast turns west."

"See you there," Willie said and hurried to his horse. It'd take him the remainder of the day to reach the village and bring Mei Ling back, Fargo knew, but he'd use the time to work out the details of the plan he'd decided upon. It was, he realized, a plan which had more chance to fail than to succeed, but it was the only one he'd been able to generate and he went into the cabin where Alberta came to him at once.

"You'll be safe here," he told her.

"Where are you going?" she asked.

"I've some best-laid plans to send astray," Fargo said.

"Tell me what you're going to do. Let me help," she said.

"You can help by staying safe here," he told her.

"You can't fight all of them by yourself," she said.

"Don't exactly figure to do that," he returned, unwilling to tell her too much. She was the kind who'd try to help regardless of what he ordered.

"What exactly do you figure to do?" Alberta persisted. "I think you owe me that much. I'm hardly an outsider in this. Don't make me one."

His lips tightened. He couldn't dismiss her demand and decided to give her enough to satisfy her. "I figure if I can get the boats emptied before they arrive there'll be a real chance to put an end to all of it," he said.

"That means you're going to the coast," she said.

"That's right. But if it goes the way I plan, I'll be on my way while they're still wondering what happened," he said. "Then, when everyone's safe, I'll go to the sheriff with you. We'll have more than enough proof to have the whole lot of them in jail."

She thought for a moment. "I still want to help," she said.

"Willie may need help here. He'll be grateful if you're on hand," Fargo said. She considered for a moment and then nodded, a trace reluctantly, and kissed him as he turned to go. He went outside to the back of the cabin and found a wooden storage box, pulled open the lid, and looked down at an array of tools, rope, bits, and pieces of cloth before he found the dynamite sticks, tied together and wrapped in a piece of canvas. He took them, strode to the pinto, and secured them in his saddle-bag before riding away.

His thoughts immediately turned to what lay ahead. For his plans to work, all the major pieces had to fall into place of themselves, he realized. The best he could do was to push some in the right place at the right time. It was the kind of task that always filled him with apprehension. He never liked projects where he had little control of his own destiny. The apprehension stayed with him as he rode and when he reached the meeting place he knew he had time before Willie would arrive. He moved into a clump of mountain ash, lay down, and half dozed until the sound of hoofbeats woke him. He rose, saw Willie approaching on the road, Mei Ling on the horse behind him, and Fargo stepped into the open.

Mei Ling slid from the horse at once as he glanced at the two young Chinese men who followed into view. "They will do whatever you want," she said, the total commitment a simple statement. She wore a light blue tunic of thin material over black, tight-fitting, knee-length trousers, both garments Oriental in cut. Her black, almond-shaped eyes met his, her finely featured face a thing of quiet beauty. "I knew you would," she said softly.

"Would what?" He frowned.

"Return to help us again. It is your *ch'i*," she said.

"We'll talk when this is over," he said, turning to Willie. "When you get the dynamite sticks, take them to the village. Show them how to use them so they can show others when they arrive."

"Got it," Willie said. "They don't take much learning, just lighting and throwing." Fargo nodded in agreement. That was exactly what he wanted, a weapon to avoid the need for marksmanship and training. He reached down, pulled Mei Ling into the saddle with him, and glanced at the two young men.

"They do not need horses. They will follow close enough," she said. Fargo waved at Willie, who was already starting back, put the pinto into a walk, and followed the trail he had mapped out. He stayed alongside the trail mostly to avoid unexpected encounters, but he saw no riders along the way, not even when he skirted the supposed way station. It was late afternoon when they neared the coast and the trees thinned out. He drew to a halt at the last line of madran, with their tropism for shorelines. The two lookouts would be somewhere in front of them, waiting, and Fargo dismounted with Mei Ling.

"Stay here," he told her as the two young Chinese men came to a halt. He left the trees in a loping crouch, his eyes sweeping the shoreline rocks and the sea beyond. There were no boats bobbing offshore, he noted, and was grateful for that. He found the two lookouts, both seated on flat rocks some twenty yards apart, both looking out at the sea. Both were in the open and he decided to wait for dark. Retreating back to the trees, he took his lariat from the Ovaro and gave it to Mei Ling. "I'll go out again when night comes. When I whistle, you bring the lariat," he said and she nodded. "But this is a step along the way. I brought you here for something more dangerous and more important," he said.

"Good," she said. "Mr. Willie told me a little of what has happened."

"I want to get everyone off the ships before the others come. I'll need you to translate for me, tell them what they must do," Fargo said.

"And these two?" she asked, gesturing to the young men seated nearby.

"They will lead the people from each boat to Han Village. They'll each take those from one boat as it arrives," Fargo explained. "You tell them what I want of them."

"I will," she said. "But there are supposed to be three boats."

"You'll take the third one. I'll go along, if I can," Fargo told her.

"That is the dangerous task you have for me?" she asked.

"Wish that's all it was," he said grimly. "I have to get aboard the boats when they come. I'll need you with me to translate to the passengers when we free them. We'll have to swim out to the first boat. You can swim, I hope."

"Very well," she said and his eyes went past the edge of the trees where night was sliding over the coast.

"But first I have to see that those lookouts don't ride back and tell Greavey the boats have arrived," Fargo told her.

She frowned for a moment in her own thoughts. "Tell me," he said.

"When no one comes to tell them the boats have started to arrive, won't they grow suspicious and come out?" she questioned.

"They will but I'm hoping that by the time they decide something's wrong we'll have everyone off the boats," Fargo said.

"If we don't?" she pressed.

"We're in big trouble," he said, pushing to his feet and starting from the trees. "Time for step one," he said as he dropped into a crouch and moved toward the rocks and the shoreline. The moon rose, affording him enough light to pick out the nearest of the two men. The lookout was still peering out at the sea as Fargo drew up behind him. A quick glance to his right showed the second lookout also peering out to the waves that rolled onto the shore. Drawing the Colt, holding it by the barrel, Fargo darted forward when he was within six feet of the man. He brought the butt of the revolver down in a short, sharp blow.

The lookout started to topple from his perch, but Fargo caught him by the collar, pulled him back, and lowered him to the ground. It had taken perhaps ten silent seconds and Fargo turned to the second lookout and began to move toward him in a crouch. Coming at him from the side made it riskier, Fargo knew, and he'd almost reached the second lookout when the man's sixth sense kicked into action. Triggered into sudden alertness, the man's head swiveled and saw the figure coming toward him. Fargo saw him start to reach for his gun and he flung himself forward in a leaping dive. His left fist shot out at the same time and the blow caught the man alongside his jaw. The figure slid from the flat rock, hit the ground, and tried for his gun again. Fargo's kick caught him in the shoulder, and sent him tumbling to one side.

Before he could recover and bring his gun up, Fargo's Colt crashed down on the top of his head and the man collapsed into consciousness. Fargo rose, whistled, and Mei Ling and the two young men appeared. He waved and they saw him and hurried over. She handed him the lariat and after binding the two men hand and foot, he let the two young men drag them into the trees. He followed and peered at the lookouts. Both were unimportant hired hands, he saw. But they had some sixty of the same kind, men hired to follow orders and not think about what they did. Mei Ling sat down beside him, and brought a package of chicken from inside her tunic, and as he ate with her he saw the two young Chinese men busily enjoying something that looked to be berries, nuts, and vegetables.

They had all finished eating when Fargo stiffened, his ears, always tuned to sounds in the distance, caught an unusual noise. He recognized it at once, the sound of canvas flapping as sails were lowered, and he jumped to his feet. Standing at the edge of the trees, he saw the vessel as it dropped anchor close to shore, a three-masted fore-and-aft schooner. "Will they come ashore?" Mei Ling asked.

"Doubt it. They'll wait for their buyers to arrive," Fargo said. "They'll look for some kind of signal but they'll wait if they don't get it. We'll do our own waiting, till they settle down for the night." He turned into the trees, saw that the lookouts had regained consciousness and had both been gagged. When two hours passed, he drew his shirt and trousers off, set them alongside his boots, and strapped his gunbelt on over his shorts. "Time to go swimming," he said to Mei Ling. She nodded, walking close beside him through the darkness. Only when she reached the shore did she take off the tunic and the black trousers. He took a moment to enjoy the piquant, upturned breasts, the slender willow-wand loveliness of her. He hadn't forgotten the beauty of her. He just hadn't expected it to sweep over him so forcefully. He also caught the tiny, smug smile that touched her lips as she stepped into the water, her pink bloomers quickly darkening from the water.

Fargo slid into the sea beside her, swimming slowly

with long, silent strokes that hardly broke the surface of the water. His eyes swept the schooner as he drew closer, and saw a lifeboat on its davit on the side nearest him, the port side. A lamp hung from the mainmast and afforded a weak glow that lighted only the immediate portion of the deck. He saw no sentries on the deck and reached out, touched Mei Ling's shoulder. She followed his gaze to the rope ladder that hung from the side of the vessel, nodded, and swam toward it with him. He started to climb up the swaying ladder first and paused at the rail, his eyes sweeping the deck before he clambered onto the ship. Mei Ling followed, leaping lightly onto the deck, her breasts bouncing in unison. He grimaced inwardly. He hadn't thought about her being such a beautiful distraction.

He put his lips against her cheek. "Take a look belowdeck but be careful. See if you find what we think we will," he whispered. "I'll meet you back here." She left to move toward the hold and he crossed to where he saw a flicker of light from the forward cabin. Voices drifted to him when he reached it and he recognized the Portuguese tongue at once. He slid to the edge of a cabin window and saw four men, one in a captain's uniform. A bottle of brandy rested on a small table in front of them. He drew back, returned to the deck, and Mei Ling climbed from the hold and hurried to him.

"They are shackled, all just like the ship I was on," she said. "One was awake. He saw me, an old man. I spoke to him. I asked him how many in the crew."

"Good going," Fargo said.

"The captain and fifteen men, he told me," Mei Ling said. Fargo's eyes narrowed for a moment. The schooner was not a big ship and didn't require the men a square-rigger would need. Fifteen was a skeleton crew but they could handle it. The information was probably right. Slave traders would want as small a crew as they could get by with. The smaller the crew, the fewer to divide the profits with and the fewer tongues to wag.

"We unshackle the prisoners, first," Fargo said.

"How?" Mei Ling frowned.

"With the keys," Fargo said. "You go back belowdeck. Wake them all up and tell them we're here to set them free. Then wait for me."

"What are you going to do?"

"Get the keys to the shackles," Fargo said, watching her hurry off, her little rear hardly moving. He went back to the forward cabin and heard that the voices had grown louder. That meant they were consuming more of the brandy. He settled in beside the rail of the ship, invisible in the dark shadows from the foremast. Though the Colt was in his hand, he wanted no shots, no noise, not until it was time. The voices continued and grew still louder. They were celebrating. *Bastards. It'll be a short celebration,* Fargo swore inwardly. He had only another half hour to wait when the cabin door opened. One of the men, short and stocky, a mate's stripes on his sleeve, emerged from the cabin, swayed, and started a weaving walk down the deck. Moving with quick, silent steps, Fargo crossed the deck and pushed the Colt into the back of the man's neck.

"The keys to the shackles," he hissed. The man half turned, fighting through the haze of brandy surrounding him, fear slowly pushing aside surprise in his eyes. He fumbled with his jacket, got it open, and Fargo saw the keys on his belt. He yanked them into his hand and smashed the gun into the man's head all in one motion. He left the figure on the deck. They'd find him soon enough but it wouldn't matter. The wheels were being set into motion. The time for caution was past. Moving forward, Fargo lowered himself belowdeck and saw the faces looking at him, hope mirrored in each pair of brown eyes. He began to unlock the shackles of each man, Mei Ling moving at his side. When he finished, they stood up and rubbed circulation back into their legs and arms. "Ask them where the crew sleeps," Fargo said to Mei Ling.

"Belowdeck under the forward cabin," she translated for him.

"Tell them to be quiet and follow me," Fargo said and started to climb from the hold. The men came after him as he led the way onto the deck and gestured to the rows of belaying pins that lined both rails of the ship. He took one of the half-wood and half-iron pins in one hand, made believe he was throwing it and Mei Ling added words to his actions. The men moved, spread out to both sides of the ship and took hold of the belaying pins that ordinarily held rigging ropes wrapped around them. Again, Fargo whispered commands and Mei Ling translated and the men lined up along both rails, each now holding one of the heavy belaying pins. They had understood and they waited, some dropping to one knee. Fargo stayed pressed against the port rail, raising the Colt as the cabin door opened.

The three men came out, the captain behind them. They weaved unsteadily, stepped forward, and halted as they took a long moment to focus on the body on the deck. Jostling each other, they knelt down at the unconscious mate, muttered, looked up, whirled, and drew guns from their jackets. Fargo held one hand up to the men, the gesture telling them to hang back, as he raised the Colt and fired, three quick shots. The three men went down together, hitting into each other as they fell in a heap. Fargo saw the captain half run, half dive back into the cabin. He held his fire, half lowered the Colt and in moments, heard the shouts from belowdeck. Another moment more saw the crew charge up onto the deck, most still in their underwear, some carrying knives.

Fargo signaled, flung one arm forward and belaying pins filled the air from both sides, a hail of the deadly little clubs, each entirely capable of splitting a man's head open. The crew halted and tried to duck away from the belaying pins that rained down on them. But the angry men weren't satisfied to just throw their new weapons. They leaped forward and rained blows down on the men who had made them captive, tortured, and tormented them. Only minutes passed when the deck was strewn with bloodied and lifeless bodies.

But Fargo's eyes were still on the cabin and he was ready and waiting when the door flew open again. The captain came out, a heavy-barreled European rifle in his hands. He started firing as he charged forward. But he only got off two shots. Firing from one knee, Fargo's single shot found its mark. The captain staggered, took another step, and toppled facedown on the deck, the rifle rolling from his lifeless hands. Fargo rose, his eyes sweeping the men, who looked on silently, most still holding belaying pins in their hands. "Tell them we're taking them from the ship," Fargo said. "Tell them this part's over."

Mei Ling spoke and the men nodded gravely. Fargo's eyes held on the lifeboat hanging from its davits. He motioned to a half dozen of the men and they followed as he climbed up the rigging ropes, and they helped him lower the lifeboat into the water. Mei Ling went with him on the first trip to the shore. "They wait here," Fargo said and she conveyed his order. It took three more trips to ferry everyone to shore and he took four men back with him, had them throw the lifeless bodies of the crew and the officers down into the hold. He closed the hatch shut and they rowed the lifeboat back, beached it, and Fargo led the way into the trees.

Mei Ling had picked up her dry clothes, he saw, and when they reached the trees he handed her a towel from his saddlebag. She went off alone, dried herself, and returned dressed. "Pick one of the men you brought with you," he told her. "Tell him he's to take everyone to Han Village and to start now. When morning comes, he's to get off the trail and stay in the trees." Mei Ling translated, choosing one of the two young men she'd brought, and Fargo watched the silent procession start to move from the coast. Most of the men bowed to him as they passed and he returned the gesture with as little awkwardness as he could. Soon they were gone, out of sight and sound. The remaining young man curled up by himself in the trees. Fargo stretched out and Mei Ling folded herself beside him. "A good beginning," he muttered. "If our luck holds we'll have those on the other boats in Han Village before Greavey and the others come looking."

"Let us say tonight was a good omen," Mei Ling murmured. He smiled at her confidence and wished he could share in it. He closed his eyes and slept, heard her lie down beside him. He rose when the first daylight slipped through the trees. Taking two of the dynamite sticks from his saddlebag, he went to the lifeboat and was easing it into the water when Mei Ling joined him. "What are you doing?" she asked.

"Preparing," he said.

"For what?" she questioned.

"I'm not sure but a lot of noise can cover a getaway," he said. She stepped into the lifeboat as he rowed to the ship, and went around to the starboard side that faced away from the shore. He weighed one of the dynamite sticks into the hole for the anchor chain, put the other one amidships under the rail. He rowed back and this time, with Mei Ling helping, pulled the lifeboat into the trees out of sight. He let the two lookouts get up, went behind a tree with them, and stood guard as they relieved themselves. When they finished, he brought them back, bound, and gagged them again.

"Your time's up," the one said before he was gagged. "They don't hear from us, they'll come."

Fargo didn't answer, aware of the truth in the man's threatening prediction. But he could only wait and hope that time would play itself out in his favor as it had last night. He rested, let himself wonder if Willie had delivered the dynamite sticks to Han Village and if Alberta was there helping him. Mei Ling, with her sensitivity, felt the apprehension that lay over him and stayed quietly at his side. The day drifted into the afternoon when she rose, stood at the edge of the trees, and peered at the shoreline. "What are you thinking?" he asked as he came to stand beside her.

"What will happen when the second ship comes," she answered. "They will see the first ship, see nobody on it."

"I'm hoping they'll think the sale was made, the slaves taken away, and buyers and sellers went out to celebrate," Fargo said. "That way they'll wait for the buyers to come back for the second sale. They won't sail away, not after having brought their cargo all this way. They'll wait, counting their money beforehand."

"But we do what we did last night," she said.

"That's the idea. I hope it goes as well as it did last night," he said.

She cast a long, sideways glance at him. "But that's not what you're really worried about," she said and he had to smile at her acuity.

"Bull's-eye," he said. "I'm worrying about the next ship being delayed. If it comes after Greavey and the others are here waiting we're finished." He turned away, the thought stabbing into him, echoing the lookout's warning. Mei Ling's voice called after him.

"You can stop worrying about that," she said. He spun, went to the trees, and halted beside her. The ship appeared from around a high rock offshore. A three-masted barkentine this time, two of the masts carrying square-rigged sails, he noted as he watched the vessel come closer to shore. The ship lowered her mainsail, then the foresail and the flying jib and dropped anchor only a few hundred yards from the schooner. He could see the crew on deck making the lines and shrouds fast as the sun began to dip into the horizon. His eyes narrowed as he swore softly. The ship was bigger than the schooner, the crew had to be larger. Suddenly to repeat last night was to be certain of failure. He needed to do something else.

Fargo spun on his heel and strode to the two lookouts tied and gagged. He pulled the gag from one, took the double-edged blade from its calf holster and rested it against the man's throat. "I want some answers and don't play games with me. You're part of a bunch of stinking slavers. I've no problem ridding the world of you," he growled and saw the man swallow hard. "There had to be some sort of signal when the ships arrived. What was it?" He pressed the knife harder against the man's throat.

"The lamp," the man said in a hoarse half whisper.

"What lamp?" Fargo questioned.

"Kerosene lamp. It's by the rocks where you saw us," the lookout said. "If we raise it three times it means they're to come ashore. We raise it once it means they're to wait."

Fargo drew the knife away and put the gag back over the man's mouth. He turned, looked past Mei Ling, who stood by watching, as did the young Chinese man. The sun was over the horizon, dusk already shrouding the land. "Wait here," he said, and stepping from the trees in a low crouch, he made his way to the flat rocks, trusting the dusk to hide him from anyone watching from the ship. It took him a few moments but he found the kerosene lamp and, staying in the crouch, returned to the trees as night fell. A plan had already formed in his mind. He had to go with it. There was no time to examine others.

"I'll spell it out to you," he told Mei Ling. "You tell him." He gestured to the young man and she nodded. Taking the big Henry from its saddle case, he handed her the rifle and gave the young man his Colt. "I'm going to take the lifeboat into the water before the moon comes up," he said. "Give me fifteen minutes, then light the lamp and give them the signal to come ashore. You heard what it is."

"Raise it three times." Mei Ling nodded.

"They'll lower a boat and row ashore. As soon as they reach the beach, you start firing at them. Don't worry about marksmanship, just throw lead at them," Fargo said. "They won't know what's going on but they'll know something's wrong and head back for the ship. I expect the captain and most of his crew will be in the boat and far enough away from the ship. That's all I want." Mei Ling nodded and Fargo went to the Ovaro and took a stick of dynamite from the saddlebag, carefully wedged it into his gunbelt, and slowly left the tent.

In the still moonless night, he found the lifeboat where they'd hidden it, pushed it onto the sand and into the water, every movement slow and deliberate, the dynamite almost throbbing at his waist. He rowed slowly, took the dynamite from his waist, and placed it on the floor of the lifeboat, holding it in place with one foot. Circling around the bow end of the schooner, he rowed toward the barkentine, slowing before he got too close. He was stopped in the water, his eyes on the shore, when he saw the lantern raised and lowered three times.

He heard the voices from the barkentine, shouts in Portuguese and then the sounds of a lifeboat being lowered into the water. He stayed in the shadow of the stern of the schooner and watched the boat leave the barkentine. It was crowded, he saw in satisfaction, most of the officers and crew in it. He began to slowly row again and came up against the side of the schooner that faced the shore and rested there in the deep shadows of the ship's hull. The rifle fire erupted from the shore and Fargo heard the shouts of surprise and consternation from the small boat. He saw the boat turn and the oarsmen begin to frantically row back toward the ship.

Taking a long match from his pocket, Fargo waited for the boat to come a little closer, lit the end of the dynamite, and stood up as he flung the explosive into the air. He saw it execute a high arc, then plummet down toward the lifeboat. It wasn't more than a dozen feet over the boat when it exploded. The night grew bright with a fiery ball of flame and he glimpsed bodies and pieces of lifeboat sailing through the air. He was already rowing back to the shore before the fireball died out and only an eerie silence followed. Mei Ling saw him as he reached the shore, and ran toward him, the rifle in hand. The young man followed with the Colt. Fargo took both weapons. "He waits here," he told her and she spoke to the young man, who stepped back.

Fargo rowed toward the barkentine, handed the oars to Mei Ling as he neared it, and took the big Henry in his hands. He peered at the ship. Two figures were standing at the rail, both raising rifles. He fired first, two shots delivered with the superior range and accuracy of the Henry, and both figures jerked as they fell from beside the rail. Mei Ling continued to row as Fargo's eyes swept the ship. But no one else appeared and the only sound was the slap of water against the boat. The scent of dynamite still hung in the air, sharp and cutting, as they came against the barkentine.

He climbed the ship's ladder first, swept the deck with the rifle ready to fire. But there was no movement and no sound and he motioned for Mei Ling to come up. "I'll look belowdeck," she said.

"I'll check the captain's quarters," he said. He quickly found the small stateroom on the stern deck and saw what he'd come for—the set of keys on the table. He hurried amidships to find Mei Ling.

"Same as the schooner, only more young girls, women, and families," she said, following him belowdecks, where he began to open the shackles. He counted some fifty people when he'd finished and by the time they had rowed everyone to shore, dawn was beginning to break. He gestured to the young Chinese man.

"Take them to Han Village. Stay in the trees soon as it's light," he said. Mei Ling spoke and the young man nodded, speaking to the others and once again a strange little procession began to snake through the trees along the trail. "Not how they planned to arrive but better than the way somebody else planned for them," Fargo commented.

He pulled the boat into the trees again as the first rays of sun touched the shore and went into the dark cool of the trees and lay down. "Only one more," Mei Ling said. "Everything has gone well. It is time to stop worrying."

"It's never time to stop worrying," he said, and then he closed his eyes and slept. He felt her beside him, her hand in his.

8

It was past noon when he woke, rose, and walked to the sea to wash. Mei Ling followed soon after and he watched her as she stood naked in the water, her lithe willow-wand body coated with tiny drops of water, the tiny little triangle even smaller when wet and pressed against her pubic mound. She could have been a sea nymph suddenly and mysteriously risen out of the depths and he was almost awestruck by the quiet beauty of her. He wanted to go to her, take her in the softly lapping waves of the beach. She wanted that, too, her every movement both chaste and sensuous, a contrast only she could somehow produce.

But he didn't go to her. Suddenly Alberta swam into his thoughts and he felt strangely uncomfortable, as though the thought of her was somehow destroying something pure and beautiful. It was a feeling he'd never felt before and he knew he couldn't explain its meaning. It had been a flash, Alberta already gone from his thoughts, yet it had been terribly real. It was as though watching Mei Ling naked before him again, made everything else seem impure. Annoyed with himself, he pushed away the strange moment, dried himself, and tossed a towel at Mei Ling.

He was in the trees and dressed when she returned, clothed in the tunic and trousers as though a sea nymph had been improperly costumed. "Who takes the next boatload to the village?" she asked.

"We do," he said.

"I will like that," she said simply, her black eyes warm and direct. "We have been alone and I have not come to you. Only because the time has not been right," she said.

"No, it hasn't," he agreed and wondered why the right time had never been so important to him in the past. It was her, he murmured to himself. She had a way of putting a different face on everything. She brought some dried berries and nuts from her pocket, a small bag of them, and they were eating together when he heard the hoofbeats outside. He strapped on his gunbelt, stepped from the trees, and saw the horseman halted, staring out at the sea and the two boats. The man, a ruddy, belligerent look to him, frowned at him.

"Who are you?" he asked.

"Just passing through," Fargo said.

"You see two men waiting here?" he asked.

"Nope," Fargo said. "Why?"

"None of your business," the man snapped, frowning as he peered out at the boats. "Don't see a damn person on them," he muttered. "I don't like this." He started to wheel his horse around.

"What's wrong?" Fargo asked innocently.

"I don't know but I'm going to tell my boss. He sent me out to check on things," the man snapped as he put the horse into a gallop. Fargo's hand went to the Colt but halted, and he left the revolver in its holster as the man rode from sight.

"He's from Greavey. He'll be back with all of them," Fargo said to Mei Ling.

"Why didn't you stop him?" she queried.

"If he didn't return they'd really get suspicious. This way he'll bring them all back here. They'll see the boats, wait, wonder, maybe just do nothing for a spell. That'll all take time and I want to give them time to get ready in the village."

"What do we do, get away from here before they come?" she asked.

He turned at the sound at his back and saw the ship slowly sailing toward the shoreline. He'd been wrestling with his answer but he'd no need to any longer. "We can't turn our backs on them," he said as Mei Ling stared at the vessel. "We'll have a few hours to free them, get them ashore, and start for the village. We've got to take it."

"Your decision," she said. He swept the vessel as it dropped anchor, some two hundred yards from the other ships. It was a ketch that had been converted into a trader and a prison hold built belowdeck, he was certain. But it was essentially a small coastal vessel and he wondered how it had survived the trip here. Luck, he decided. Much smaller than the other two vessels, its crew would be the smallest, also.

"We don't have any time to waste," he said to Mei Ling. "I'll have to move fast, coldly, brutally." He glanced at her to see her reaction. Her beautifully featured face showed only an Oriental imperturbability.

"Brutal people bring on brutal ends," she said, nodding to the ship.

"Let's get the lifeboat," he said and went to the trees. She helped him push the boat into the water and climbed in with him as he lay the rifle on the floor.

"Shall we signal them with the lantern?" she asked.

"No. I want them uncertain of us," he said and handed her the oars. He sat back as she rowed and leaned forward to her only as she neared the ketch. A man in an officer's uniform looked down from the rail. He was joined by a man wearing a captain's cap and a half-dozen crewmen. All watched the rowboat approach. "Wave and smile," Fargo said. "I want them wondering who the hell we are." He waved vigorously. Mei Ling waved between strokes, and flashed them a wide smile. Fargo's hand stole toward the big Henry under his seat as he saw the captain raise a hand for them to halt.

"No closer," the man called in a heavy Portuguese accent.

"Keep rowing," Fargo whispered as his hand closed around the rifle.

"No more," the captain called again, his voice rising, a note of nervousness in it. Mei Ling glanced at Fargo and his eyes told her to keep rowing. Suddenly he saw what he'd been watching for. The two crewmen at the end brought up rifles but they were the only two. Fargo whipped the Henry from beneath the seat, firing as he did, the two crewmen with the rifles his first targets. They went down as one and he swung the Henry to the right, firing as fast as the repeater rifle would fire shots. The men at the rail toppled as though they were ducks in a shooting gallery. All but the captain, who managed to turn and run. The lifeboat came against the ketch and Fargo grabbed the rope ladder, pulled himself up it to the low rail, and jumped down to the deck.

He saw the captain at the bow of the ship, coming out of a small cabin. The man held a ring of keys in his left hand, a heavy pistol in his right. His shot was wild and Fargo fired, the heavy rifle slug catching the man in the upper torso. He spun as he staggered, fell against the opposite rail of the ship, and hung there for a moment. Fargo heard the scream come from his lips as he saw the ring of keys fall from the man's hand and go over the rail. He leaped for the rail but heard the small slap of water as the key ring plunged into the sea. "Shit," Fargo bit out, slamming his fist against the rail. "Goddamn." Mei Ling climbed onto the deck as Fargo pushed the captain's body with his foot. There were no other keys on him.

He ran to the small cabin from which the man had come and tore through everything in the little stateroom. There were no more keys and he returned to the deck cursing and saw Mei Ling come up from the hold. "Same thing, some forty people," she said.

"Only we won't be unshackling them with keys," he said, striding past her and beginning to peer into every small room and section of the ketch. He found what he sought in a small room, not much larger than a closet, at the rear of the vessel. The toolroom held hammers, pliers, chisels, saws, sail repair tools, and a variety of other shipboard tools. He chose a heavy steel saw, a hammer, and a chisel and returned to where Mei Ling waited. "It's all we have," he said as he followed her to the space below the deck where the passengers were shackled to iron rings.

He tried the chisel and hammer, first, Mei Ling holding the chisel against the shackle as he brought the hammer down on it. But the smooth, round surface of the shackle made the chisel slip off it each time. But he found that he could saw an indentation just deep enough for the chisel not to slip out of. When he smashed the hammer down, the chisel snapped the shackle in two. "That's it," Mei Ling said.

"It'll take us hours," he bit out and saw her face grow sober. "We don't have any choice," he added and went to the next man. The saw took time and he cursed as the time seemed to stand still. But there was no way to speed things up, no way to free the prisoners except by this slow, steady process. Greavey and everyone else were riding hell-bent to reach the coast, he knew, and he felt the perspiration coat his brow inside the heat of the closed space. But finally he split open the last shackle of the last man and he rose. His back and arms ached as he climbed onto the deck. Mei Ling explained what was going to happen to the freed passengers, which included six women. He took turns with Mei Ling rowing them to the shore and the day was moving toward an end when the last of them were ashore and into the trees.

Greavey and the others had to be near, he knew, perhaps only minutes away, certainly not more than a half hour away. "Get started. Stay off the trail," he told her. "They'll be riding too hard. They won't be looking for anyone."

"You're not coming, are you?" she said, her eyes on his. "You're staying."

"Maybe I can give you some more time," he said. "All they'll know is that their slave labor is gone. They won't know where. The more I can keep them busy the more time you'll have to reach the village."

"No. Come with me," she said. "You have given enough of yourself."

"Get moving," he said gruffly. "Hurry." She turned from him but not before he saw the pain in her eyes. He waited, watching the last procession move away until the forest closed them from sight. He took the Ovaro from the trees, led the horse down to the shoreline and south to where a cluster of madrone grew almost to the line of rocks that touched the sea. He returned on foot, halted opposite the ships and swept the rocks until he found a pair that formed a hollow V between them. He wedged himself into the V of the rocks and settled down to wait. He had no plan. There was none to make. He'd have to play it by ear. The important thing was to delay Greavey and the others as long as he could and give himself a way to flee. He cast a glance at the waves behind him, only a half-dozen feet away. The sea might prove his way out, he realized. He savored the thought. It would be fitting. It had all started with the storm at sea. It should end with another.

The sound came to him, the ground vibrating with the pounding of hooves and he peered out from inside the rocks. The horsemen came into sight minutes later and he saw Greavey, Sam Bundy, and Bart Egan in the forefront. Their hired hands spread out along the shoreline as everyone halted and peered at the ships. They frowned at the silence and the emptiness of the coastline.

"What the hell do you make of it?" Sam Bundy asked.

"They wouldn't leave, walk off," Greavey said. "Something's happened."

"There's a lifeboat beached over there. Somebody get out to the ships," one of the Gallardes said. He dismounted and took five of his men with him to the lifeboat. Fargo watched them row to each of the ships, searching each and finally rowing back. He smiled at the time it had taken. "The captain and crew of the barkentine are gone, no place at all. The crew on the other two ships have been killed. The goddamn Chinese got loose somehow. They're all gone now, not a goddamn one of them anywhere," Gallarde reported.

"That's crazy," Bart Egan cut in. "Where would they go? They don't speak English. They've got no money. It doesn't make any damn sense. And how'd they all get loose?"

"Maybe it doesn't make sense but they're gone, that's for sure," Greavey said. Fargo frowned as he saw Frank Dussart and Joe Ebert walking slowly from the water, studying the ground.

"They went this way, into the trees. Their tracks are all over," Dussart said. Sam Bundy and a few others joined him in following the tracks into the trees and Fargo swore silently. He heard the shouts from inside the trees and the men emerged with the two lookouts. The two men fell over their words in their haste to tell what they knew and Fargo saw Sam Bundy's face harden, Bart Egan and the others doing the same.

"One son of a bitch was behind it, big, rode an Ovaro," one of the men said.

"Fargo," Bundy bit out.

"Never got his name but he did it. Had a China girl with him," the one lookout said.

"The bastard." Greavey growled.

"The last of them left about an hour ago, maybe a little more, all except him," the man said.

"What happened to him?" Bart Egan asked.

"I don't know but he didn't leave with them," the man said.

"He's still here," Sam Bundy said. "I can feel the bastard. He's here." He turned and yelled at the men who were lined up in the background. "Start searching this place, every goddamn inch of it. Start with the trees and work your way to the sea."

The riders broke into small groups and faded into the trees back from the shore. Fargo's lips pulled back as he cursed. They'd come to him eventually. Maybe not so eventually, he muttered as he saw Greavey and Sam Bundy dismount and start to move along the rocks near the shore. His glance went to the sky. It'd be dark soon. But not soon enough, he told himself as the men came from the trees and searched the open land. He'd be found, and he'd have no way to flee without a hail of bullets slamming through him. But they'd question him, first. They wanted information. He'd buy more time for Mei Ling and the others.

Now his way, Fargo muttered as he saw Greavey wander away from the others and start to pass near the two rocks where he hid. He'd come back again, in further, come onto the hiding place, Fargo knew. Watching Greavey pass, he suddenly darted from the rocks and was behind Greavey before the man heard him. He pushed the gun against Greavey's head as he knocked the man to his knees. Greavey's cry brought heads turning. "Back off or he's dead," Fargo called.

He saw Bundy, Bart Egan, the Gallardes, and the others start to come toward him. Fargo let the hammer of the Colt click as he drew it back. "Back," he said again through gritted teeth.

"Jesus, do what he says," Greavey croaked. The others halted and took a step backward.

"Where are they?" Sam Bundy asked. "Let's deal. Tell us where they went and you can walk."

"They went off on their own, all over the countryside. You'll never find them," Fargo said.

"You're lying to us," Bart Egan said.

"Never." Fargo laughed, pulling Greavey to his feet and backed the man toward the water, keeping the gun pressed into the back of his head. "One step this way and he's dead," Fargo said, directing his next words at Greavey. "You're going to find out if they're really friends," he said.

"You some sort of preacher, Fargo? You going to give up living for a bunch of Chinese nobodies?" Bundy tossed out.

"Nope," Fargo said. "It's something called principle. The idea of a man being free, not owned. It's something you wouldn't understand. But you'll understand this. You come after me and he's dead and so are at least six more of you. Count on it."

He saw Bundy and Bart Egan exchange glances, the Gallardes joining in, uncertainty in their faces. He was so intent on keeping the Colt on Greavey and watching the others, he never heard the figure behind him until he felt the gun press into the back of his neck. "It's over, Fargo. Pull the gun back and drop it," the voice said.

Fargo felt the frown tear deep into his forehead. He was making a mistake, hearing things, he told himself. It couldn't be. The gun pushed harder into his neck. He pulled the Colt from Greavey's head and the man dove forward and turned, fear still wreathing his face. Fargo let the Colt slide from his fingers and felt it hit the ground against his foot. He turned and stared into the hazel eyes. Once again, shock waves swept through him. He felt as though he'd been physically assaulted. The world was suddenly a place where nothing made sense, a place that turned upside-down and back again without end.

"Make me understand," he murmured. "Tell me I'm not mad."

"God, it took me forever to get here," Alberta said almost casually, but there was nothing casual in the pressure of the gun into his neck. "Your friend Willie is a damn mother hen. He stayed with me every damn minute. Finally, he went off to Han Village and I got away," she said.

"They took you a prisoner. They found out you were working with Sheriff Yancey," Fargo said.

She gave a little laugh. "The first part's true. I made up the second part. I had to tell you something that'd make you believe me."

"It was a lie, all of it," Fargo said and felt the fury rising up inside of him.

"All of it. I was always working with Sam and Bart and the others," she said.

"Why'd they have you tied, a prisoner?" He frowned.

"We had a falling out," Alberta said. "They tied me up to scare me, make me come around to their thinking." She cast a glance at Greavey. "Right, Ed?"

"More or less," Greavey conceded.

"We had an arrangement. I was to get twenty-five percent of their profits for helping them. I changed that to fifty percent. What I did was worth it. They wouldn't agree."

"We tied her up to let her cool off and think for a few days. Shit, we didn't know you freed her," Greavey said.

Alberta's eyes went to the others in a quick glance. "Fifty percent," she said. "You want your slave labor. I can tell you where they are. Fifty percent."

The others exchanged glances and mutters, and finally Sam Bundy spoke up. "Damn you, girl," he growled. "Fifty percent if you really know."

"I know," Alberta said triumphantly.

Fargo felt the fury inside him become a massive rage that filled every part of him. She'd played him for an absolute fool for the second time and the second time was worse than the first. He wouldn't let her destroy everything, tell them what they desperately wanted to know. "You bitch," he hissed at her. "You rotten, lying, evil bitch. You can't tell anybody the truth. You don't know what it means to tell the truth." He turned to Greavey and the others, took in Bundy, Bart Egan, and the Gallardes. "She's going to lie to you. She doesn't know where they are. I changed where they were taken."

"Goddamn liar. I saw them on their way there," Alberta shouted.

Fargo shook his head stubbornly. "You only thought you did. I changed the place. I wrote it on a piece of paper. You let me go and I'll give it to you," Fargo said to Greavey and the others. "Hell, I can't win now."

"It's a deal. Where is it?"

"An Indian name. I put the piece of paper in my boot," Fargo said and dropping to one knee, he reached to take off his boot.

"He's lying, can't you see?" Alberta screamed at Greavey.

"Shut up, Alberta. We want to see what he has," Sam Bundy said. Fargo's hand shot up from his boot to the calf holster. He yanked the blade out and thrust it upward in a short, lightninglike arc. It went into Alberta's wrist and the gun fell from her hand as she screamed. He spun her around, the knife to her throat as he slid backward, keeping her in front of him.

"You don't want to shoot a lady, do you? Not gentlemen like you and not a lady who can tell you what you want to know. Shoot her and you'll never find out," Fargo said, edging to the water with Alberta.

"You bastard, Fargo. You stupid bastard," Alberta hissed at him.

"I'm saving your damn neck," he told her.

"Hell you are," she said.

Sam Bundy's voice cut in. "He's the only one who really knows. Shoot her. She's in the way," he said. Fargo swore. He had misjudged the total dishonor among them. Alberta spun and as she faced him, he saw the pure hatred in her eyes. Four shots rang out and Alberta shuddered in his arms. Her eyes closed and pulled open again, and the hatred was still in them. He saw the deep breasts heave as, with her last breath, she pulled a scream from inside her.

"Han Village," she cried out and fell against him, her eyes closing for the last time.

Fargo flung himself backward into the sea as Alberta's limp form slid from him. He hit the water, rolled, and rolled again through the waves. A half-dozen shots rang out, hitting the sand and the water. "Fuck him," he heard Greavey shout. "We got more important things to do." Fargo lifted his head from the waves and saw the riders had turned and were charging off into the last of the day. There was only one place they were going. He pulled himself from the surf and ran across the short strip of sand and scooped his Colt up and ran again, this time along the beach to where he had left the Ovaro.

He vaulted into the saddle and gave chase, staying behind just far enough to hear the thunder of hooves. Catching Greavey and the others would only get him killed, he knew, and he watched the night descend, following the horsemen along the trail he had mapped for them. The night had deepened when they turned from the trail and onto the road that led to Han Village. Fargo turned from chasing their tails, riding parallel to them in the forest, cutting to the right. He was opposite the slope of Han Village when the riders turned into it and charged up the long slope. He saw Greavey, Bundy, Bart Egan, and most of the others slow almost to a halt and let their men attack. The village was silent, no one stirring, not a light anywhere. Mei Ling and the last boatload couldn't have reached the haven more than a few minutes earlier, he estimated.

The riders started to spread out to the small houses. They drew their rifles and started firing. Fargo's eyes lifted and he was the first to spot the thin sticks of dynamite arching through the sky from behind the houses on both sides. They looked harmless, as though they were twigs borne by a sudden, strong wind. But when they exploded, the night opened up in a red-and-yellow flame that enveloped everything. Fargo felt the shock wave and the wind that swept over him. Screams of men and horses began and ended almost instantly. Dropping to the ground, glad he had hung back where he was, he saw Bart Egan and Sam Bundy trying to flee.

He pulled the big Henry from its saddle case and fired. Both men went down and stayed down. The Greavey brothers were next, clinging to their horses as they started to flee. They toppled from their mounts with Fargo's next two shots. He spied two of the Gallardes and put an end to their ruthless business. Rick Dennison didn't need a bullet. He was crawling on legs that would never work again, his body drenched in red. The Eberts supported each other as they staggered away. He saw Sam MaComber riding away. He had been lucky. He was untouched. Fargo changed that with a last shot.

The terrible explosions had died away. Many of the thin houses would have to be rebuilt but Fargo saw the people moving down the slope, stopping to embrace each other. He glimpsed Han surrounded by a group of the boat people. Strolling forward, leading the Ovaro, he found the slender figure running toward him. She came against him and clung to him. When she lifted her head she had a tear and a smile. They seemed to fit perfectly together.

He put her on the Ovaro and slowly rode from the village. When he found an arbor by a stream in a cluster of red alder, he spread out his bedroll. Her sweet, willow-wand nakedness was against him in moments and he realized he felt like a man who had tasted too much of a succulent fruit that had risen to sicken him with its ripeness and he was reminded again that many inviting things are deadly. The slender body pressed into his and he knew the meaning and healing of purity.

"I knew you would return for me," she murmured. "It had to be."

The wisdom of the Orient, he murmured silently. It was everything he'd heard. And more.

LOOKING FORWARD!
The following is the opening
section from the next novel in the exciting
Trailsman **series from Signet:**

THE TRAILSMAN #207
CHIMNEY ROCK BURIAL

Nebraska, 1860
Where the shadow of Chimney Rock
falls on the graves of many early
settlers of the West . . .

Skye Fargo's presence in Council Bluffs, Iowa, was unplanned. His intended location had been Omaha, but his Ovaro had picked up a stone bruise on the hoof of his left foreleg. Council Bluffs had been the closest town and Fargo had walked the stallion there.

As it turned out, Council Bluffs not only had a blacksmith, but a vet. The blacksmith removed the horse's shoe and the vet took a look at him. He pronounced the animal fit, but said he would need at least a week for the bruise to heal.

That had been five days ago and Fargo was starting to go stir crazy. Even though he'd met a woman while in town, that only took care of his nights. His days were spent walking around town, or sitting in front of his hotel, going to the saloon when it opened. He'd exchanged more words with the bartender at the Buckhead Saloon than he had with anyone in months.

He was on his way to the Buckhead Saloon when he saw a woman being buffeted back and forth among three laughing men, across the street in an alley. It was the fact that it was happening in an alley that caused him to cross over. Also, the woman was calling for help.

As he got closer he could see that she was an attractive woman in her early thirties. On the other hand, the men were all in their twenties. He didn't know who had a beef with whom, but three men against one woman made it easy for him to pick sides.

"Please," the woman was saying, "stop . . . someone help . . ."

One of the men had just pushed her toward another when Fargo elbowed him aside roughly, bouncing the man off a wall. As the man slid to the ground, stunned, Fargo approached the other two.

"Okay, fun's over," he announced. "Leave the lady alone."

Fargo was taller and wider than all three of them, but up close it was easy to see that they were drunk.

"Get lost, mister," one of them said. "This ain't your business."

"Please, sir," the woman said, "help me. Get me away from these men."

"Forget it, mister," the second man said. He was holding her by the shoulders. "This is my girlfriend."

"You're a little young for her, aren't you, son?" Fargo asked.

"Well, you're too old for her," the man replied.

"Never mind," Fargo said. "Just let go of her and there won't be any trouble."

"You're the one lookin' for trouble," the first man said. "Why'd you hit my brother like that?"

"Son—" Fargo said, but he stopped when he saw a familiar look in the young man's eyes. "If you go for that gun, friend, I'll have to kill you. Is it worth your life to have a little fun at this lady's expense?"

The man on the ground began to stir and rise. Fargo took one step and kicked him in the head just hard enough to stun him again.

"Jesus, mister," the second man said, "stop hittin' our brother."

"Let the lady go."

"We didn't mean no harm," the first man said.

"Okay," Fargo said, "no harm done. Let her go, pick up your brother and move on."

The two men exchanged a look, and then the first one nodded and the second one let her go.

"Come on, Richie," they said, helping the other man to his feet.

"What happened?" he asked.

"We'll tell you later," the first man said, and then they walked off, supporting him between them.

"Are you all right, miss?" Fargo asked.

"I think so," she said. "They didn't really hurt me, but I was getting dizzy."

"Why were they doing that to you?"

"I don't really know," she said. "I approached them to ask them for help, but they seemed to prefer . . . pushing me around."

Fargo took a moment to look at her. The way she dressed spoke more of the East than the West. The dress would have looked fine at a tea party with its ruffles and such, but it was out of place on a dusty western street.

She had dark hair that had been pinned up on her head, but tendrils of it had been shaken loose by the treatment she'd received. She was really quite pretty, with blue eyes and pale skin and a very appealing cleft chin.

"You look like you could use a drink," he said.

"Oh, I don't indulge, thank you," she said, "but could you recommend a place for coffee or tea? You see, I just arrived on the stage."

"Why not go to your hotel?"

"I haven't registered at a hotel, yet. Can you point me towards one?"

"Is this the help you were asking them for?" he asked.

"Well, no . . ." In that moment she seemed to take a good look at Fargo for the first time. "Perhaps you can help me, though."

"Well, the nearest hotel is—"

"No," she said, "I mean with my problem."

"Your problem?"

"Yes," she said. "Would you have some time to listen to me?"

"Miss," he said, "it just so happens all I have is time."

*   *   *

The lady introduced herself as Grace Viola. Fargo escorted her to the nearest hotel, where she was able to secure a room. They then went into the dining room, where she ordered tea, he ordered coffee, and they both ordered some apple pie.

"What brings you to the West, Miss Viola?" he asked.

"It's Mrs.," she said, then added, "I'm a widow."

"Oh, I'm sorry. A recent widow?"

"Fairly recent," she said. "My husband was a minister in Philadelphia. He died some months back."

"And you decided to come out West?"

"Actually," she said, "I don't like the West very much. I didn't like it the first time I was here."

"And when was that?"

"About twelve years ago," she said. "I was a young woman then, newly married. My husband then—not the same man, mind you—decided we should come West. We got this far and joined a wagon train, but no sooner had we started our trip across Nebraska than he fell prey to a snake bite."

"He died?"

"Yes."

Fargo thought that this woman didn't seem to have much luck with husbands.

"Then what happened?"

"Well, I went on with the wagon train but . . . I was pregnant, you see. Eight months along."

"Your husband took you on a trip of that nature while you were that pregnant?"

"I'm afraid so."

"What happened?"

"What you would expect," she said. "I went into labor early, and the child—a boy—did not survive."

Jesus, he thought, if this woman didn't have bad luck she'd have no luck at all.

"What happened then?" This was the most interesting conversation he'd had in days.

"Well, some folks were kind enough to bury the child and then stay behind with me while I recovered. By that time, however, I had decided to return East. The West had taken enough from me."

"How did you get back?"

"Well, the people who stayed with me wouldn't go back, but before long a wagon did appear going the other way. Another family who had suffered a loss also decided to turn back, and they were kind enough to take me with them."

"This is quite a story," he said.

"Yes, I suppose it is," she said. "I returned to Philadelphia and it took me quite a while to recover mentally from my double loss."

"I can imagine," he said. "You're to be commended for recovering at all."

"Well, I did, but it was still quite a long time before I met another man I thought I could love."

"Your minister husband?"

"No," she said, "another man who managed to get himself shot before we could marry. I met my husband—the minister—when he presided over my fiancé's funeral."

Fargo was starting to wonder if all of this was true. How could one person experience all this hardship?

"I see."

"I fell in love with him eventually, and we married. We lived together for six years before he, too, died."

"Violently?"

"No," she said, "he fell ill and simply passed on."

"I'm sorry."

"So you see, I had to make this trip back here."

Fargo frowned.

"Uh, no, I guess I don't see, Mrs. Viola."

"Please," she said, "call me Grace."

"All right, Grace," he said. "Why do you feel you had to come back West? And back here?"

"Well, I have no family back East," she said.

"They died, too?"

"My parents died when I was quite young," she said. "I was raised in an orphanage. In fact, that's where I met my first husband. He and I both grew up there and when we were old enough we left together and were married. You see, no one ever adopted us. When a child gets to a certain age—well, most people want small children, to raise as they see fit."

"I see."

The story—if completely true—got sadder and sadder by the moment.

"Zackary—my first husband—insisted he wanted to come West . . . but I've been through that."

"Yes," Fargo said. "We were talking about why you would come back here."

"Yes, we were."

She put her teacup down and placed her hands in her lap. She stared very solemnly across the table at Fargo.

"Mr. Fargo, my child—my only child—is buried out there. You see, once I lost him I could no longer have children."

Fargo was now surprised that this woman had not taken her own life long ago.

"Now that my husband is gone I want to find my child and give him a proper burial."

"After all these years?"

She nodded.

"It's something I feel I have to do . . . in here," she said, clasping her hands to her breast where her heart was.

"Well, I suppose that's understandable," he said, and he was about to wish her luck when she spoke first.

"Can you help me find that grave?"

It was then he knew he should have minded his own business.